# ELEVENTH HOUR

**S. Hussain Zaidi** is a veteran of investigative, crime and terror reporting in the Mumbai media. He has worked as resident editor at *Asian Age*, Mumbai; and editor, investigations, at *Mumbai Mirror*, *Mid-day*, and the *Indian Express*. He is the author of several bestsellers including *Black Friday*, *Dongri to Dubai*, *Mafia Queens of Mumbai* and *Byculla to Bangkok*. His latest work is *Dangerous Minds*. Several of his books have been adapted into movies including the eponymous *Black Friday*, directed by Anurag Kashyap; *Shootout at Wadala*, based on *Dongri to Dubai*, directed by Sanjay Gupta; and *Phantom*, based on *Mumbai Avengers*, directed by Kabir Khan.

Zaidi is also associate producer for the HBO movie *Terror in Mumbai*, based on the 26/11 terror strikes.

## Also by the author

*Byculla to Bangkok: Mumbai's Maharashtrian Mobsters*

*Headley and I*

*Mumbai Avengers*

# S. HUSSAIN ZAIDI

# ELEVENTH HOUR

HarperCollins *Publishers* India

First published in India by
HarperCollins *Publishers* in 2018
A-75, Sector 57, Noida, Uttar Pradesh 201301, India
www.harpercollins.co.in

2 4 6 8 10 9 7 5 3 1

P-ISBN: 978-93-5277-929-1
E-ISBN: 978-93-5277-930-7

Typeset in 11/14 Adobe Devanagari at
Manipal Digital Systems, Manipal

Printed and bound at
Thomson Press (India) Ltd

*For Gautam Mengle, my friend and protégé*

# 1

*Thursday morning, New Delhi.*

Raju Kanaujia was a happy man. His wife was at her parents' house with their two sons. His neighbour was out of town for three months. And his neighbour's wife was sending him feelers with increasing intensity. He had decided that he would string her along for a couple of days more before paying her a visit to ask if he could 'borrow some milk'.

As he went about his job, cleaning the washrooms at the Ministry of External Affairs' premises, he mentally calculated how much money he had left. Affairs were expensive. Even a cheating housewife would demand to be pampered. If he wanted to get into bed with her, an occasional gift was a must.

Due to his preoccupation, he almost missed the flurry of activity as he exited the general washroom on the second floor. Almost. Kanaujia watched curiously from the washroom door as a short, portly man in a sherwani and fur cap came stumbling

1

out of the conference room, one hand to his face, surrounded by a ring of guards and diplomats. It took a minute or two to recognize him. The man was none other than the guest of honour for that day's function!

Like a majority of smartphone users, Kanaujia's instinct was to shoot first and ask questions later. Quickly, he slipped inside the general washroom, held the door open by a crack and pulled out his cellphone as the bunch of men drew closer. As they passed by the door on their way to the executive washroom, Kanaujia captured a perfect frame of the Pakistan high commissioner stumbling by, blood streaming from his nose, crying like a child who had been beaten up by the school bully.

What Kanaujia saw was the culmination of a series of events going as far back as 26 November 2008, when ten terrorists stormed the city of Mumbai and stripped it of its pride. For sixty hours, Indian security forces fought valiantly while everyone else watched helplessly.

Superintendent of Police Vikrant Singh, an Indian Police Service officer from the Maharashtra cadre, was among them. Then a deputy commissioner of police with the Anti-Terrorism Squad, Vikrant was in his office in Nagpada, completing the paperwork on a module of the Indian Mujahideen that he had busted two weeks earlier after months of hard work, when the phones and the wireless started going crazy. For the next ten minutes, he could scarcely believe what he was hearing. At the eleventh minute, he had rushed out of his office, pistol in his holster and spare magazines in one hand, and fishing out his car keys with the other.

Over the next two days, at the Oberoi-Trident hotel, Vikrant exchanged bullets with terrorists hell-bent on destroying the city he loved and saw many of his comrades, senior and junior alike, fall prey to their fire. After the National Security Guard finally stormed the hotel and finished the battle, a bruised, grimy and supremely infuriated Vikrant got into the first police vehicle he saw, drove to the Colaba police station around the corner and locked himself inside the Detection Room. One of the four constables manning the police station, who happened to be passing by, heard a series of loud thuds from within.

Even as he was debating whether or not to raise an alarm, the door opened and Vikrant walked out, his face expressionless, blood dripping from the knuckles of his right hand. He walked away without so much as looking at the constable, who rushed into the room. On the far wall was a freshly formed pit flecked with blood.

Locking himself in one of the washroom stalls, Kanaujia examined the photo he had taken. *The man is clearly someone important.* Kanaujia had seen him being brought to the building amidst tight security and a lot of very important people rushing to receive him. He racked his brains and finally remembered what the canteen fellow had told him about the cultural programme slated for that evening. It was a ghazal performance to promote friendly relations between India and Pakistan.

He studied the picture again. The left side of the man's face – the part not hidden by his hand – was definitely swollen and beginning to turn purple. Thanks to the 13-megapixel camera and the ample lighting in the corridor, the photo was amazingly clear. Who the hell was he? Maybe Google could tell him...

Soon after 26/11, Vikrant, thanks to the IM module bust, was transferred to the Intelligence Bureau on deputation, something he had always wanted. He threw himself into the world of surveillance and monitoring like a man possessed, using all his source-building and investigation skills with the sole motive of preventing another 26/11. He found a mentor in his reporting head, Inspector General of Police Shahwaz Ali Mirza, who was not only an intelligence pro but also had keen insight into the way the mind of a radicalized Muslim youth worked.

After four years with the IB, Vikrant was transferred to the Delhi bureau of the National Investigation Agency, another outcome of 26/11. Two years later, Mirza too was transferred to the same bureau as Vikrant's immediate superior. Both devoted themselves to investigating terror-related incidents and gathering strong evidence against terror accused.

But the wounds of 26/11 never really healed. For nine years, Vikrant had watched in helpless fury as the Indian government kept sending evidence to Pakistan, and Pakistan all but spat on the files. At the same time, both governments kept talking about nurturing friendly relations, promoting harmony and similar rubbish.

Which was why, when he learned that Pakistan High Commissioner Zakir Abdul Rauf Khan was going to be the guest of honour at the MEA's concert to promote friendly relations between India and Pakistan, Vikrant had immediately asked Mirza to arrange a personal meeting with the diplomat.

'Absolutely not!' Mirza had thundered. 'I'll be damned if I'm letting you anywhere near the Pakistani high commissioner, with all that fire over 26/11 still burning inside you!'

'Please, sir,' Vikrant said. 'I just want to talk to him.'

'Yes, and I am the shah of Iran.'

'With you, I can believe that,' Vikrant replied, tongue in cheek. Mirza had to laugh. The number of identities he had assumed when he was a field agent for the Research and Analysis Wing were legendary.

After a minute's silence, Mirza looked at his protégé thoughtfully.

'This is important to you, son?' Mirza asked softly.

'It is,' Vikrant asserted.

'I'll see what I can do. But I'm coming with you. Clear?'

And so it was that half an hour before the concert, Vikrant and Mirza had walked into the conference room where Khan was greeting the other guests. Mirza introduced Vikrant as 'the talented boy who has cracked all those cases', and Khan came forward with a big smile on his face.

'Mashallah!' he said, placing one hand on each of Vikrant's burly shoulders. 'We need people like you, beta. The world is in short supply of honest and dedicated men like you.'

'Thank you, sir,' Vikrant said. 'I hope I am not the only one who dreams of a day when the work I do will no longer be required.'

'Ah, but you see, beta, there are so many forces of evil working against people like you and me,' Khan said sadly.

'As long as we have each other, right, janaab?' Vikrant said, smiling. Only Mirza knew that Vikrant hardly, if ever, smiled. He stiffened a little.

Khan smiled back. 'Alhamdulillah!'

'So, does this mean we can expect some progress regarding 26/11, sir?' Vikrant asked.

'Boy…!' Mirza warned, but Khan, unaware of what he was walking into, stopped the veteran spy.

'No, no. It's okay. He is an investigator and this is a question he will naturally ask. You see, beta, the thing with democracy is that it has to take its own time.'

'Its own time, as in, nine years?' Vikrant said sardonically.

'Nine, nineteen, ninety. As long as necessary. Verdicts should be based on evidence, not sentiment, or else how are your country and mine any different from the military rules that we condemn, don't you agree?'

'So you are going to stick to that, sir?'

'That is my nation's stand, beta. And hence, it is also mine. Till such time as we are shown concrete evidence, this will have to be our stand,' Khan said, smiling condescendingly.

Vikrant chuckled. Mirza felt a tremor inside him.

'You find something funny, barkhurdaar?' Khan asked.

'Just the fact that I had come here hoping to appeal to your finer instincts. To plead for justice for all those who died and who were left broken that night. They deserve closure, if nothing else.'

'And why do you find it funny?'

'Because now I know that there's only one way to deal with you people.'

Khan turned to Mirza, who was, in his mind, begging for the diplomat to shut his bloody trap before it was too late.

'Mirza sahab, our young friend is still at an age where he lets emotions get the better of him. It is up to us to forgive him, as life will soon teach him…'

The others in the room never got to know what life was going to teach Vikrant because at that very instant, Vikrant drew his right hand back and swung it with all the force he could muster, delivering a resounding blow on Khan's left cheek. The force of the burly hand, coupled with eight years of pent-up rage, sent the short, portly diplomat careening into a table laden with sandwiches and cookies, on which he landed face first, breaking his nose.

An hour later, Kanaujia was dialling the number of a local Hindi newspaper that he regularly read.

'I have something big,' he told the harassed reporter who answered. 'I want to know how much you're willing to pay for it.'

# 2

*Thursday morning, Bhopal.*

Usman Qureshi smiled to himself as he walked out of his cell in Bhopal Central Jail. It was hot outside but the heat hardly bothered him. His mind was somewhere else.

As the prison guard unlocked his handcuffs, Qureshi eyed the four men already assembled in the yard. One was doing push-ups, while the other three were walking briskly. Grinning at them, he stepped forward to enjoy the one hour of exercise the prisoners were granted as respite from solitary confinement, rotating his wrists and stretching his shoulder muscles.

Qureshi came to a halt some distance away from Mazhar Khan, the one doing push-ups, and started stretching. Khan caught Qureshi's eye and winked.

Qureshi turned towards his other three brothers-in-arms. Shaukat Asad was now sitting on the floor and doing yoga. Before the guard could notice, he quickly raised three fingers of his right hand slightly and then let them drop on his knee. Only Qureshi saw this gesture, and he gave the slightest of nods in return.

Mustafa and Ibrahim Kadir, who were brothers, were doing sit-ups in tandem in one corner of the yard. As they raised their torsos, both of them gave Qureshi a quick thumbs-up before going back down. Qureshi smiled.

'Mashallah!' he said.

The prison guard looked at him.

'Such a beautiful day, isn't it, saheb?' he said to the guard, who continued to stare suspiciously.

Around twenty nautical miles off the coast of Somalia, three small motorboats waited patiently, anchored a few metres away from each other. There were five burly Somali men on each. It was well past 1 a.m. and they had been waiting for the last two hours.

None of them showed any signs of impatience or restlessness. They had been told beforehand that they would have to wait a while. 'We might even call it off if it's too risky. Wait till 2 in the morning and go back if nothing happens. Come back twenty-four hours later,' were their instructions.

And hence, the fifteen Somalis, dressed casually in shirts and denims and sneakers, sprawled around their boats, munching on chips, sipping from cans of beer and smoking cigarettes.

'You think it's happening tonight?' one of them asked.

'We wait and we watch, man,' his friend replied.

'Yo!' a third called from another boat. 'Over there.'

Everyone looked in the direction indicated by their friend. They could see lights in the distance that were growing brighter. As the freighter came closer, the men on the boats started getting up. Packets of chips were crumpled and stuffed in pockets, cans of beer were tossed out and cigarettes were either stubbed out or stuck between their lips as the men collected their knapsacks.

Several rope ladders were already hanging from the side of the freighter as it drew up alongside the three boats. Four men from each boat clambered aboard while the remaining three turned the motorboats around and zoomed away into the night.

The twelve who had climbed aboard were met by a stone-faced man dressed in black combat fatigues who, without uttering a single word, walked over to four of them who had smoldering cigarettes in their mouths. Calmly, he plucked each cigarette from their lips and tossed them overboard. The men exchanged looks but no one protested.

# 3

The impact of Vikrant's slap was felt not only on Khan's chubby face, but in a lot of other places over the following days.

The immediate outcome had been the diplomatic nightmare for the Ministry of External Affairs. Within half an hour of the incident, the Pakistani prime minister was on the phone with his Indian counterpart, having a heated exchange of words. The Indian prime minister, after slamming his phone down so hard that it almost broke, took a minute to calm down and then called the union home minister.

The home minister, after slamming his own phone down ten minutes later, had immediately ordered a central government inquiry against Vikrant Singh.

In another corner of the national capital, a pagemaker with *Dainik Awaaz*, a local Hindi daily, gleefully put the photo of Pakistan High Commissioner Zakir Abdul Rauf Khan, looking tearful and bleeding from his nose, being escorted from outside the conference room at the MEA building, while Raju Kanaujia happily counted the money that the reporter had given him.

'It would be a good idea to disappear for a while,' the reporter told him.

The next day's edition of the paper got sold out within an hour. Pictures of its front page started circulating on social media and before noon, several national channels were bidding for the picture. The editor of *Dainik Awaaz* waited patiently as they outbid each other and ultimately sold the photograph to a leading news channel.

An hour later, even as the inquiry against Vikrant progressed, the same photo began flashing on the channel, with the headline claiming to have the 'inside story' of what really caused the ghazal programme to be called off. There was another round of furious calls from Pakistan to India and the verdict on Vikrant was decided even before the inquiry had started.

The information and broadcasting ministry tried to intimidate the news channel into taking off the photo, which they had put up as a permanent display on one half of the screen while the news anchor raged on relentlessly beside it. The same anchor revealed, on live television, how the government was trying to pressurize their channel and proclaimed that they would not 'bow down to the whims of a government that is getting as dictatorial as it is irresponsible'.

In the middle of the storm that was raging around him, Vikrant Singh sat calmly in a small cabin in the MEA building, chewing gum and reading a novel from Peter James's Roy Grace series. After Vikrant had slapped Khan, a furious Shahwaz Ali Mirza had pounced on him, dragging him out of the conference room and into the cabin with a strength and ferocity that surprised his junior.

'Fucking stay there!' Mirza growled before walking out, slamming the door shut behind him.

Two hours later, when Mirza returned with a couple of Special Protection Group personnel to take Vikrant into custody, they found him sprawled out on a chair, dozing.

As the furore over his actions heightened, Vikrant spent the next three days under house arrest while his fate was decided by the top bureaucrats of the country.

On the fourth day, Vikrant was back in the same cabin, waiting to be summoned into the inquiry, reading the fourth novel from the same series.

The door opened and he looked up to see Mirza enter the room. He closed the door behind him and sat down heavily on a chair.

Before his mentor could open his mouth, Vikrant said, 'I'm sorry, sir.'

'You bloody well should be,' Mirza snapped.

Vikrant shook his head.

'Not for what I did,' he said. 'For the trouble I caused you. If I know you – and I like to think I do – you must have moved heaven and earth in the last three days for my sake. I'm sorry for that.'

Mirza sighed. 'Why, boy? Why throw away a career over this?'

Vikrant shrugged. 'Some things are worth it.'

It was Mirza's turn to shake his head.

The door opened and an SPG officer looked in.

'They want him in there,' he said curtly.

The inquiry, which everyone in the room knew was a mere formality, was presided over by Principal Secretary Aninda Das of the MEA. Also present were representatives from the Union Ministry of Home Affairs and the Maharashtra Home Department, and a retired director general of police.

'Vikrant Singh,' Das began, glaring at the cop over his spectacles. Vikrant felt an urge to stick his tongue out.

'You are facing an inquiry for assaulting the Pakistan high commissioner while he was on a visit to India, and thereby jeopardizing the already strained relations between the two countries. We have, over the last few days, taken the testimony of several witnesses and they concur that you hit His Excellency Zakir Abdul Khan without provocation. You have now been summoned so that you can present your defence.'

Vikrant took a deep breath before speaking, and Mirza silently prayed to Allah to ensure that the lad did not make things worse for himself.

'With all due respect, sir, I do not think my actions warrant a defence,' Vikrant said.

After a minute's silence, Das asked, 'You want to explain that?'

'I have a scar on my arm, sir. A scar from a shrapnel wound I sustained while defending my city, and my country, on 26 November 2008. I look at my arm every morning to remind myself of that night. And while countless people like me relive that night every day, there are others who think it is funny to throw words like "due process" and "democracy" every time someone asks for justice.'

Das glared. 'Young man. We are all fully aware of the horrors of those three days. It is a matter of great shame for all of us. But that doesn't give you the licence to go around hitting diplomats. Nor is this panel interested in your emotional speeches.'

'I understand, sir. I plead guilty.'

Vikrant made this statement so casually that everyone in the room stared hard at him for a minute.

'You heard me, sir,' Vikrant said.

Das nodded. 'So be it. SP Vikrant Singh, you are hereby…'

At that moment, the door flew open and two men ran inside, sweating and puffing. One of them went straight to Das and whispered urgently in his ear. Das turned around to look at the man, then blinked several times, digesting the information. The bureaucrat then waved Mirza over.

Vikrant watched curiously as Das, in turn, whispered in Mirza's ear and Mirza started smiling. When he was done talking, Das looked sharply at the veteran spy over his glasses.

'You find something funny, Mr Mirza?' he inquired.

'No, sir,' Mirza said quickly and walked over to Vikrant, still smiling.

Before Vikrant could ask him anything, Das said, 'Mr Singh, you are placed on suspension pending further notice. Mr Mirza will tell you the rest.'

Vikrant watched as everyone filed out of the room till only Mirza and he remained.

'What?' Vikrant asked.

'If I didn't know better, I'd suspect you had arranged this,' Mirza chuckled.

'What?' Vikrant repeated.

'That Indian Mujahideen module you busted back when you were with the ATS? The terrorists broke out of Bhopal Central Jail this morning. The PMO wants you on the case "only as a consultant" immediately.'

# 4

The breeze ruffled the old man's silky white hair as he stepped on to the deck of the cruise liner. He smiled, feeling the warmth of the sun on his face. The cruise liner had left Mumbai half an hour ago and was on its way to Lakshadweep for a full tour of the islands and Abdul Jabbar Hakimi, while well past the age to be childishly excited, was definitely looking forward to the trip.

As he walked down the top deck, he glanced at his co-travellers. He had already become friendly with a young woman of thirty, who was travelling alone.

'Careful!' Hakimi cautioned as a couple of kids ran past him, laughing loudly. There were thirty passengers in all on the cruise liner. It was a mixed group, ranging from children to people his age, and the atmosphere was festive.

Hakimi came to a halt against the railing where a man, casually dressed in cargoes and a t-shirt, was standing, smoking a cigarette and looking out at the sea.

'*Itne gaur se mat dekhiye, bhaisahab,*' Hakimi said, smiling. '*Samundar ko nazar na lag jaaye.*'

The man turned his head towards Hakimi and stared at him unblinkingly for several seconds, slowly exhaling smoke through both nostrils. Hakimi raised both hands in a 'just kidding' gesture and quickly walked away. He did, however, turn around and steal one last glance at the man, taking in his predatory stance and tattooed, muscular arms.

As Hakimi rounded a corner and reached the open-air lounge, he came face-to-face with Vaishali, the woman he had befriended. She was stretched out on a deck chair, dressed in a t-shirt and slacks, reading a book. She looked up and smiled at him. He sat down on the deck chair next to her.

'You can lean back on them, you know,' she said, laughing.

'Age, beta.' Hakimi grinned. 'There weren't many of these around where I was born and I'm too old to start learning new sitting positions.'

Vaishali laughed again.

'Why are you here alone?' she asked curiously. 'I mean, no children, grandchildren…?'

Hakimi nodded. 'Typical stereotype of an old man on a vacation,' he said. 'Babysitting his grandchildren while his children have fun.'

Vaishali's curiosity deepened. 'You say that like there's something wrong with it,' she said.

Hakimi shook his head. 'I just chose a different life.'

'What, you're alone?'

'We're always alone, beta,' he said.

She shook her head.

'Now you're being a stereotype of the wise old man,' she chided.

Hakimi smiled.

'I'm not married. Nor have I adopted a child,' he said.

'Would you mind if I ask…'

'Why?' Hakimi sighed. 'Sometimes, things happen that leave a lasting impact on you, and all the advice about moving on doesn't help. For me, it was the death of my parents. I grew up alone and by the time I was grown up, I began to like it.'

'You mean, you began to find it safer,' Vaishali said.

Hakimi gave her a sharp look. She smiled sadly.

'I pretty much grew up alone myself,' she said.

Hakimi waited and she went on.

'My father was never around and my mother was so busy making sure my needs were met that there was hardly any interaction between us. It was only in her later years that we began to get close.'

'She's no more?' Hakimi asked gently.

Vaishali nodded, staring out at the sea.

For a while, neither of them spoke. Then she said, 'This is my first vacation after I lost her last year. Part of my healing process, I think.'

But Hakimi was only half listening. The muscular man had just come into view, and Hakimi noticed him taking a good long look at him and Vaishali before slowly walking away.

# 5

*Monday afternoon, Bhopal.*

'Did any of them ask for a new toothbrush over the last couple of months?' Vikrant asked the superintendent of the Bhopal Central Jail.

'I … will have to find out,' the flummoxed SP stuttered, looking at his deputy, who seemed equally clueless.

'Please do,' Vikrant told him. 'I think you will find that at least one new toothbrush was requested, and not more than two months ago.'

Vikrant and Mirza, along with SP Devendra Kumar and DSP Sameer Khare, were standing in the isolated cell block where the five IM members had been lodged before their escape twenty-four hours earlier. The cells were lined up on the left, adjacent to a narrow corridor for the guard to patrol. A chair was placed near the access door to the cell block and there were windows in front of every cell.

After learning about the jailbreak from Mirza, Vikrant had hastily packed a bag and run into a waiting SUV, which had raced to the airport. Tickets had already been booked for him and Mirza on the first available flight to Bhopal, and they were received by local NIA officers as soon as they landed in the afternoon. Another SUV was waiting to take them to the prison. Vikrant had had to duck to prevent being photographed by the press as they drove through the prison gates. The PMO had made it very clear that he was to maintain as low a profile as possible.

Vikrant now walked the length of the cell block, staring at the five cells. He stopped at the last one and walked inside. The other three men were behind him.

'You thinking what I'm thinking, lad?' Mirza asked.

Vikrant nodded.

'A toothbrush can be fashioned into a key,' he said, looking all over the cell. 'It's painfully slow work, scraping it into the right shape bit by bit, and can take up to a month. What were their bathing arrangements?'

'There is a row of bathrooms only for high-security prisoners. Each one would be escorted to and from there separately every morning. Same for using the toilets. Once every morning and later on request,' DSP Khare said.

Vikrant nodded. 'They stole soap from the bathrooms. They'd only need small bits to insert into the lock and get a mould of the levers. Soap is pretty malleable when damp. Using that, they scraped a toothbrush into a key while using the toilet.'

'With what?' Kumar inquired.

Vikrant shrugged. 'Even the edge of a tap would do,' he said.

The SP swore and nodded at Khare, who ran out to follow up.

Vikrant moved from cell to cell, examining each one carefully. 'They just needed to open one cell door. I'm guessing it was Mazhar Khan. He's the burliest, and the most vicious.'

Mirza nodded and continued, 'So, the bugger waited till the guard had walked past his cell, opened the door and pounced. It would have taken less than a minute, especially if he'd practised opening the lock.'

'The guard's neck had been snapped,' Kumar offered. The two veterans nodded in unison.

'And the guard had keys to all the cells?' Mirza asked.

Kumar responded in the affirmative.

'Why was there only one guard to patrol the cell block?' Vikrant queried.

Kumar looked sheepish. 'Manpower issues. Plus, it's a small block, with a separate access, and two guards patrol the outer passage,' he said, nodding in the direction of the passage beyond the door leading to the cell block.

'And the guard inside the cell block had the keys to the access door as well?'

Kumar's face reddened. 'Yes.'

'Must have been smooth sailing once the guard in the cell block was down. Take his keys, free the others, open the access door...' Mirza said.

'And they had the guard's gun too,' Vikrant finished, heading to the outer passage.

In their statements, the guards in the outer passage said that the prisoners had grabbed one of them at gunpoint and forced the other to surrender his weapon. The outer passage led directly into the yard where the prisoners were taken for an hour of exercise every day. Once they reached the yard, both the guards were knocked unconscious.

'Human pyramid to climb the wall?' Mirza asked. The three men had reached the yard by now.

'Most likely. One of them reaches the top and ties the bedsheet to the bars. They climb up and use the same bedsheet to climb down the other side,' Vikrant surmised, looking at the bedsheet still tied to the bars.

They heard a movement behind them and turned to see DSP Khare, his face a mix of wonder and admiration.

'Mazhar Khan got a new toothbrush two months ago,' he said. 'Told the guard he had dropped his old one down an open drainpipe in the bathroom.'

'We're done here,' Vikrant said.

# 6

*Monday night, Bhopal.*

'You knew, didn't you?'

Mirza looked up from the report he was reading. Vikrant sat in front of him with an amused expression.

'Absolutely no idea what you're rambling about, boy,' Mirza said.

The two men were in the NIA office in Bhopal, planning out the next steps in their investigation. Both of them were looking at reports of the inmates' behaviour over the last six months, hastily prepared by the prison officials on their demand.

Vikrant looked sceptical.

'The jailbreak happened before dawn. You'd have got a call from someone or the other within the hour. Which means, when I was sitting in that cabin reading my novel and waiting for the inquiry to start, you had already known about it for several hours,' he said.

Mirza didn't reply.

'Also, I'm sure that whoever took the decision of deputing me to the team on a "consultant" basis,' Vikrant went on, 'couldn't have thought it up on his own. So, what really happened?'

Mirza only smiled. Vikrant took up the challenge. They had been playing this game for years now.

'I'd say you saw the opportunity to keep me from being stripped of my rank and being thrown in jail and spoke to someone in the home ministry, possibly even the PMO, I wouldn't put it past you. I don't know how you got them to agree, though, with the pressure from...'

'From the country that's been letting the masterminds of a terror attack roam around free for nine years?' Mirza asked sardonically.

Just then the door to the office opened and two DSPs came in.

Samar Goyal and Akhil Jaiswal were part of the Special Investigation Team set up by the home ministry to investigate the jailbreak. Headed by Mirza – Vikrant was pretty sure the old man had purposely put himself at the helm – the team had an abundance of resources at its disposal, including personnel, equipment and funds, along with carte blanche to cut through red tape.

'What's happening, lads?' Mirza asked.

'We have local railway police watching train stations, while also scanning CCTV footage of the last twelve hours. Toll plazas on highways have also been informed and the police are searching all buses heading out of the state,' Jaiswal said.

'Buses will be too risky,' Vikrant responded. 'They'll want to lie low, and possibly they'll have fanned out to rendezvous at a pre-decided point. But I'm willing to bet they're already out of the city by now, because they had to have known we would search every corner.'

Goyal nodded. 'I'm in touch with officers from almost every police station in the city, who're giving me hourly updates of their search operations. Plus, there are nakabandis and surprise checks happening everywhere.'

Vikrant and Mirza exchanged glances. Vikrant turned to Goyal.

'Get in touch with the Bhopal police commissioner and ask him for any cases where a vehicle has been stolen or forcibly taken in the last twelve hours. If they managed to get vehicles early enough, they could have easily driven out of the city.'

Next, Vikrant addressed Jaiswal. 'I'm giving you a list of known relatives and friends of all five. Get our local officers to start checking whether any of them have been in touch. If they didn't have outside help, they're going to reach out to someone or the other for money, if nothing else.'

Jaiswal nodded.

'Are we listening in to known IM members and affiliates?' Vikrant asked Mirza, referring to the suspects in India whose phones were tapped by the IB.

Mirza nodded.

'Okay, I'm going to talk to some of my sources,' Vikrant said.

As everyone turned to their respective tasks, Mirza's cellphone beeped. It was an email with a report shared by a friend in the CIA. American satellites had picked up a commercial freighter that had slowed down for five minutes for no apparent reason near three motorboats while passing through Somali waters. Mirza made a mental note to follow up with his American friend.

# 7

*Monday night–Tuesday morning, Bhopal.*

It took a good six hours for results to come, but investigative work always requires a lot of patience and doggedness. Mirza described it as 'shaking every damn tree in the yard, because where the hell else could the cats be hiding?'

The first cat fell out of a tree in Mumbai, Vikrant's old stomping ground, where he had cultivated sources after years of hard work before he was deputed to Delhi. While Mirza coordinated with central agencies and Goyal and Jaiswal worked with the local police, Vikrant called up an old informant staying in Cheetah Camp, Trombay, a huge expanse of slums in eastern Mumbai, where one of the five Indian Mujahideen men, Shaukat Asad, had grown up. His aged parents and younger brother still lived there, and Vikrant's informant, Kamran Sheikh, stayed three doors away. This was by no means a coincidence or luck.

Nine years ago, Vikrant, while making inquiries with Asad's family before and after the latter's arrest, had quietly identified the most curious among the onlookers in the area. He asked his team to speak to them and get a sense of their personalities, to see if any of them could be cultivated. Kamran Sheikh, with his lack of scruples, love for money and talent for sniffing out gossip, emerged as an easy winner, and Vikrant spent three months turning him into an informant.

When Vikrant called Sheikh, the latter had already learned about the jailbreak from the news.

'*Tension nahin, saheb*. My eyes and ears are open,' he told Vikrant.

Six hours later, Sheikh called back from a payphone in Kurla, Mumbai. It was nearing midnight, but the entire investigating team was still in the NIA office.

'Did Asad just walk into Cheetah Camp?' Vikrant asked, half-sarcastic.

'No, sir,' Sheikh said. 'But a distant uncle of Asad's, Shakeel Khan, who stays in Bhiwandi, came all the way here to meet Asad's father in the middle of the night, and left in ten minutes.'

Vikrant sat up.

'Please tell me you have more than that.'

'I'm following the uncle.'

'FUCK!' Vikrant yelled happily, and everyone in the office turned to stare. He gave them a thumbs-up sign and gestured towards his phone.

'He came by bike, and is on his way back,' Sheikh continued. 'I'm on my own bike. He stopped for a smoke so I went looking for a payphone...'

'Go back this minute! Do not lose sight of him!'

'*Tension nahin, boss*. I have his bike number. And I know his name.'

Vikrant made a mad scramble to grab the nearest pen and paper.

Half an hour later, Vikrant, using Shakeel Khan's name and licence plate number, had obtained his cellphone number and put it under surveillance. Location tracking showed the uncle reaching Bhiwandi, and Sheikh confirmed the same. Vikrant told him to turn back and not expose himself to risk any longer.

Next, Vikrant got Shakeel Khan's call records for the last twelve hours. This was when the second cat fell. Late in the evening, Asad's uncle had received a call from a payphone in Nashik. The call had lasted for a little over five minutes, and Vikrant went through all his call records for the last one week and confirmed that he had not received any other calls from there, which was a strong if not irrefutable indicator that it was not someone who usually contacted him.

Goyal was already drawing up the route from Bhopal to Mumbai online. 'Nashik is one of the cities on the way, sir,' he told Vikrant, who nodded.

'Whom do we know in Nashik?' he asked, still poring over the call records.

'The DCP of the Crime Branch is someone we've worked with earlier,' Jaiswal volunteered.

'Get him on the phone,' Mirza said.

The DCP, an enterprising officer who understood the importance of prompt action on terror-related cases (as well as how any delay on his part could affect his career) roused a team of his best officers from their beds at 2 in the morning and sent them to the payphone from which the call was made, which was in the middle of a usually crowded market where one could easily disappear.

The officers, motivated by the prospect of a positive record in the Annual Confidential Reports, woke up every shopkeeper with CCTV cameras over their store entrances as well as the payphone operator, and got them to open up their shops. They had already received pictures of the five IM members on their phones.

The payphone operator, as expected, did not remember who had made the call and did not keep records. But a jewellery store across the street from the payphone had a CCTV camera, which resulted in the third cat falling from the tree. It had captured a Tata Indica stopping near the payphone, Shaukat Asad alighting from it, making the call, getting back into the car and the car driving away in the direction of the highway leading to Mumbai.

Within the hour, the footage had been emailed to Mirza.

'Should I book flight tickets to Mumbai, sir?' Jaiswal asked.

'Why haven't you done that already?' Mirza snapped.

# 8

*Tuesday afternoon, somewhere at sea.*

The twelve Somalis were having dinner in the common galley when the man in black fatigues walked in, carrying a duffel bag. He placed it on the floor near them and walked away.

The men stared curiously at the bag. Their leader, Marco, opened the bag and cautiously dipped his hand in, while the others huddled around. He smiled as he drew his hand out, holding a shiny Uzi sub-machine gun. There were several whistles around the room as one by one, twelve Uzis were handed out.

Next, Marco took out ammunition clips, five for each gun. As he was handing the clips around, a shadow fell across the galley and they looked up to see the man in black fatigues enter the room again with a smaller duffel bag.

'Sidearms, and more ammo for the Uzis,' he said tonelessly.

'Nice,' Marco said, smiling. The man's face remained expressionless.

Over the four days that they had been on the freighter, the Somalis had quickly fallen into an easy routine. They would wake up early in the morning and go through a gruelling workout session on the deck. This was followed by breakfast in the galley, after which they were free to do pretty much what they wanted. The man in black fatigues had shown them a small hold where they could smoke, but alcohol was forbidden on the vessel. The hold quickly became their favourite place, where they would spend their days smoking and sipping soft drinks or snacking on tidbits, of which there seemed to be an abundance.

The only communication they'd had with the man in black all these days was through a wireless, when he would give them terse instructions about mealtimes or to stay below deck when an official boat passed by.

Now, as the Somalis distributed Glock pistols from the second bag among themselves, the man said, 'You move out tomorrow night. I'll have more gear for you then. Be ready.'

'Move out how?' Marco asked.

'You will be told,' the man said curtly.

'Now hang on, man,' Marco said, moving towards him, Uzi in hand.

The man looked at him curiously.

'We been here four days now and we don't even know your name. You treat us like we're some kinda insects, bossin' us around this way an' that. I gotta tell you, I don't like being treated like that.' Marco casually raised the Uzi, which he had loaded with a clip, and let it rest against his shoulder.

'So, what I'm saying is that maybe you gotta start treatin' us with a little more respect, seein' as your mission depends on

us and all. And that you might want to not treat us like shit an'
put guns in our hands at the same time, know what I'm sayin'?'
Marco continued with a smirk on his face.

The man cleared his throat before speaking. 'Well. It seems
that you asked me a question. Several, actually. The most
important being, what is to stop you from killing me now that
you are armed with sub-machine guns and pistols. Did I get
that right?'

Marco nodded.

'Can you reach into my left breast pocket, please, Marco?'
the man asked.

Marco's smile dimmed a little but he did as he was told,
coming out with a thickly folded piece of paper.

'Read it, please,' the man said. Marco nodded to one of his
soldiers, who came forward and covered the man in black with
his Uzi, while Marco unfolded the paper and went through its
contents. When he looked up, his face had changed.

'Yes, Marco. That's a list of every known family member of
yours and the rest, with their current locations. We get updates
on them every twenty-four hours. To answer your first question,
if you so much as breathe out in my direction in a way that is
not to my liking, they will all suffer. Now flip it over, please,' the
man said pleasantly.

Marco did as he was told and once again read it from top
to bottom.

'As you may or may not have guessed, that's a list of sixty
men from your own country who, like you, are experts in the
art of warfare and are available for money. So, to answer your
second question, no, our mission does not depend on you,' the

man said, taking the page from Marco, folding it and casually placing it back in his pocket.

'Which brings us,' he said, 'to your remaining question. You have been wondering what my name is, and it is my understanding that it bothers you not to know.'

Marco said nothing.

'My name is Marwan,' the man said before turning around and walking out.

# 9

*Tuesday afternoon, Mumbai.*

'How many more joining us?' Vikrant asked.

'Local police has got five men meeting us on the way. That makes twelve. Should be enough,' Goyal responded.

'We hope,' Mirza said grimly.

Mirza, Vikrant, Goyal and Jaiswal were speeding toward Palghar in an unmarked SUV. A veteran Mumbai Crime Branch constable who knew the highways like the back of his hand was driving while Jaiswal was glued to his smartphone, relaying Shakeel Khan's movements as provided by the NIA officers tracking his cellular location. In the back seat, Mirza fished handguns out of a small duffel bag while Goyal made calls, coordinating with the various agencies involved. Vikrant, next to the window, smoked a cigarette, much to Mirza's irritation.

'Two weeks of no smoking and you feel like having one exactly when I'm sitting in a bloody vehicle next to you?' Mirza said with a frown. Vikrant did not react.

The four officers had landed in Mumbai early in the morning. By the time they entered the arrival area, Mirza had received text messages from the Mumbai police commissioner, the Crime Branch chief and various officers whom he had worked with earlier, offering every possible help. There were also updates on the surveillance he had set up on Shakeel Khan, reports of his cellular location, which showed him at home, and reports from the Nashik Crime Branch DCP.

A DCP of the Mumbai Crime Branch had been waiting outside the airport to receive the four investigators. The group was on its way to the Crime Branch headquarters with the DCP at the wheel when Mirza's phone beeped. Asad's uncle was receiving a call.

'Pull over,' Mirza told the DCP, who obeyed and all the five men waited.

Five minutes later, a surveillance technician at the NIA head office had emailed a voice clip to Mirza. It was a recording of the conversation that Shakeel Khan had just finished. Mirza downloaded it and played it at full volume.

'*Salaam alaikum!*' Khan said.

'It's me.'

'*Bolo.*'

'*Palghar mein Sativli gaon jaante hain?*'

'I'll find it.'

'Take a left after Sai Mauli hotel. Leave now.'

The caller hung up abruptly after this instruction. Jaiswal started typing furiously on his cellphone. Half a minute later, he looked up and said, 'Found it. Sativli, Palghar district. It's on the Mumbai–Ahmedabad national highway.'

Mirza turned to the DCP, Ashok Mankame.

'We need weapons, men and the fastest vehicles you have, along with someone who knows the roads here and can get us to Sativli as fast as is humanly possible,' Mirza said.

Mankame turned on his siren, took a U-turn in the middle of the highway and sped to the nearest Crime Branch unit, phoning his officers to give them instructions. By the time he came to a halt outside the Unit VIII office, there was a duffel bag, two SUVs and six of his most experienced men waiting at the entrance. By then, Mirza's surveillance team had relayed to him that Shakeel Khan had left from Bhiwandi and was on the move. The Crime Branch men had quickly calculated that it would take him close to one hour to get to Sativli, while it would take them more than an hour. Mirza swore.

Now, as they all sped towards Sativli, with five men from the Palghar police also joining them, Mirza calmly gave out handguns to everyone but Vikrant.

'You're on consultant basis only, remember?' Mirza smirked. Vikrant sighed, took one last puff of his cigarette and threw it out of the window. His mentor chuckled and handed him a gun as well. Just then Mirza's cellphone rang.

'API Rekundwar, Palghar Crime Branch, sir. I'm across the street from the Sai Mauli hotel,' the assistant police inspector leading the local police team said.

'You got the details of the man I sent you?' Mirza asked.

'Yes, sir. What do I do if he gets here before you do?'

'Let him leave. Follow him but keep your distance. And only follow, nothing else. You're armed?'

'All of us, sir.'

'Not in police vehicles?'

'No, sir.'

'Not in uniforms?'

'No, sir.'

'Be careful,' Mirza said before hanging up. 'How much longer?' he asked the driver testily.

'Half an hour at the most, sir.'

'Where's the uncle?' Mirza demanded.

'He … he just stopped a little before Sativli, sir,' Jaiswal said, looking up from his phone for the first time.

Shakeel Khan fumbled in his pocket and pulled out his cellphone with a shaking hand.

'Yes?' was all he could manage.

'Stay there,' was all the caller said before hanging up.

The same conversation was heard in the SUV a few seconds later.

'Step on it,' Mirza told the driver as he dialled API Rekundwar.

Shakeel Khan had just lit a cigarette with trembling fingers when a van with tinted windows drew to a halt across the street. A man dressed in casuals, wearing sunglasses and a cap, got out and walked straight towards him. When he took off his cap and shades and came closer, Khan recognized his nephew.

'*Sab theek, beta?*' he asked.

Asad just held out his hand. Khan opened the tail box of his bike and took out the pouch that Asad's father had given him. Asad snatched it from his hands and began opening it when API Rekundwar came to a screeching halt behind the van, handgun drawn, followed by four other cops in plainclothes. Unaware that Asad had exited the van right in front of them, all five cops rushed across the street, guns pointed at Asad and Khan.

'Don't move!' Rekundwar screamed.

At that moment, the van's sliding doors opened noiselessly and four men stepped out, armed with AK-56 assault rifles.

Mirza's team realized that something was amiss long before they reached the spot. The constable at the wheel had broken every rule in the Motor Vehicles Act to get to Khan's location as fast as possible. He was five minutes away when they saw vehicles speeding in the other direction and people running away on foot. Instinctively, everyone in the SUV cocked their pistols.

Next, they heard the gunshots. Some were single shots from pistols, others were bursts from assault rifles. Mankame, who was driving the second SUV, stepped on the pedal and caught up with Mirza's vehicle. The cops had a gut feeling that something had gone wrong.

By a stroke of good luck, a sixteen-wheel trailer speeding towards Mumbai was on the road at the exact instant the armed terrorists stepped out of the van. The driver of the trailer braked hard on seeing the men with assault rifles, but his momentum still carried him almost abreast of the van, causing the terrorists to jump out of the way.

During these few seconds, Asad sprinted around the trailer and towards the van, while the policemen took position behind a row of cars parked on the other side of the street. Rekundwar had the presence of mind to drag Shakeel Khan along. 'Move once and I'll shoot you in the head,' he told the old man, sticking his gun in his face, before turning his attention to the terrorists who had, by this time, taken position behind the sixteen-wheeler while its driver crouched under his seat, weeping for his life.

Both groups started shooting at almost the same time. Two of Rekundwar's constables, who were the most exposed, went down in a volley of gunshots while the officer himself was grazed by a bullet in his arm. Clenching his teeth to ignore the pain, he emptied his clip at the terrorists and crouched behind a car to reload when DCP Mankame brought his SUV to a screeching halt right in front of him, providing additional cover. The other SUV, carrying Mirza and his team, stopped in front of Rekundwar's men. The ten cops tumbled out of their vehicles from the safe side while the other was peppered with gunfire.

In perfect coordination, Mirza and Vikrant took up positions on either side of their SUV and began shooting well-aimed rounds at the trailer. Goyal and Jaiswal followed their lead. The rest of the policemen caught on quickly and within minutes, the terrorists couldn't get a single shot off without exposing themselves to risk.

'Stop shooting!' Vikrant suddenly yelled. 'Hold! Hold fire!'

The cops stopped shooting and quickly reloaded their weapons in the silence that followed. True to his hunch, Vikrant heard the van's doors slam shut and the ignition start. 'Goyal, Jaiswal, go around the back! Mankame, with me!' he yelled as he ran round the front of the massive trailer.

As Goyal and Jaiswal rounded the back of the trailer, they almost got run over by the van reversing at full speed. It turned around in a scream of burning rubber and shot forward. Goyal, Jaiswal and Mankame emptied entire clips at it while Mirza made a mad dash for the nearest SUV. Only Vikrant saw the two delayed-action grenades that the terrorists had placed under the trailer before leaving.

'DOWWWWN!!!' he shouted as he launched himself towards Mankame, who was closest to the trailer, hurling him to the ground.

Then there was a loud bang and everything went white.

# 10

*Tuesday evening, Mumbai.*

'Is it true that the terrorists were armed with assault rifles?'

'Were any civilians hurt?'

'How did they manage to enter Palghar undetected?'

'Is it true that they set off a high-tech remote-controlled IED made of RDX with a blast radius of two kilometres after they left?'

The last question made Mirza chuckle. *The stories have already started gathering meat in the telling,* he thought as he watched the DGP Maharashtra, Paramjeet Kalra, try to quell the ever-increasing clamour of journalists at the press conference.

Mirza was in a senior doctor's office at the Kokilaben Ambani Hospital in Andheri. The two constables who were hit by several rounds in the firefight had died instantaneously. The others who had sustained minor injuries were treated at the civil hospital in Palghar. Vikrant, Goyal, Jaiswal, Mankame,

43

Rekundwar and the trailer driver were shifted to the Ambani Hospital at Mirza's insistence.

Despite several lacerations to his arms and face, Mirza spent the next hour on the phone with everyone from the NIA director to the Prime Minister's Office, shooing away doctors and nurses who tried to treat him. Finally, a doctor forcibly led him into his office and told him to use it as long as he wanted, instead of roaming through the corridors with a bleeding face.

'You're freaking out my staff *and* my patients,' the doctor said sternly. Mirza fought the urge to stick his gun in the doctor's face just for the heck of it.

Now, his face and hands treated, Mirza watched DGP Kalra field questions with thinly veiled impatience as the questions got increasingly aggressive and, in some cases, stupid.

'Is the state going to have to live with terrorists roaming free on its streets?' a journalist asked.

'I think the state is fair-minded enough to realize that two of my men laid down their lives today but did not let anyone else come to harm,' the top cop replied without missing a beat.

Mirza sighed. The press conference lasted for five more minutes, after which Kalra politely excused himself and left, the reporters still throwing questions at his back. As Mirza switched off the television, his cellphone buzzed. It was a text from his boss in Delhi.

'PMO wants me to take a press briefing of my own in two hours. Bloody hell ☹.'

Mirza grinned. The man was two ranks and ten years his senior, but used emojis with an abundance rivalled only by teenagers. Exiting the doctor's office after taking his permission, Mirza went over to the private ward where all the five cops were admitted.

Jaiswal and Goyal, being farthest from the trailer when it exploded, had been thrown forward due to the impact of the blast. Goyal had ended up spraining his wrist and a ligament in his shoulder as he landed sideways, while Jaiswal had landed on his back and suffered whiplash, but miraculously did not break any bones. Both were sedated and asleep.

Rekundwar, apart from the wound he had sustained when the bullet grazed his arm, was fine. Mankame had twisted his ankle when Vikrant had tackled him to the ground. He had been discharged after a check-up but was hanging around in the hospital room out of concern for the others. Vikrant had taken most of the damage. One side of the trailer had blown off when the two grenades went off under it, and a large piece had dug itself into the back of Vikrant's leg. Additionally, a lot of shrapnel from the grenades had embedded itself into various parts of Vikrant's body, and the doctors had had to operate on him for over two hours to get all of it out.

In spite of everything, when Mirza walked in, Vikrant was awake.

'The anaesthetic wore off an hour ago and he won't let me sedate him,' the nurse said helplessly.

'He will,' Mirza told her as he sat down on a chair next to Vikrant's bed.

'How many dead?' Vikrant asked, sounding weak.

'Two constables. The ones from Palghar,' Mirza said, his voice equally tired.

'What about the trailer driver?'

'He's in the ICU. Internal bleeding and a lot of broken bones.'

'What's his name?'

'Dashrath Pandey. Native of UP. Started working as a driver here around five years ago.'

'Family?'

'Wife. Two kids.'

'What was his fault?' Vikrant asked and Mirza winced.

'His fault was that he was in the wrong place at the wrong time, lad,' he said heavily.

'No, sir. His fault was that we failed.'

Mirza was at a loss for words.

'All of us. As a system. We failed to make the streets safe enough for Dashrath Pandey to be able to do his job without risking his fucking life,' Vikrant said, staring at the ceiling.

'We did,' Mirza said sadly. 'But now we will set that right.'

'Will we, sir?'

'I know I won't rest till I have. Will you?'

Vikrant tried to shake his head but winced. Mirza waved the nurse over.

'Sedate the boy, will you?' he told her, standing up.

'Wait,' Vikrant said.

The nurse sighed. Mirza stared at his protégé.

'They didn't need money,' Vikrant continued.

'What?'

'They had a vehicle and they had AKs. Someone was already providing them with everything they needed. Which means that Shaukat Asad didn't seek out his uncle for money,' Vikrant said, thinking hard.

Mirza asked the nurse to give them a minute and sat down.

'Whatever it was,' Mirza said, 'it was important enough for Asad and the others to risk coming out of hiding.'

'And to come armed with assault rifles to get it. What's the uncle saying?'

'Asad's father gave him a pouch, which he handed over to Asad. He didn't open it.'

'Of course,' Vikrant said sarcastically. 'He's in custody?'

Mirza nodded.

'We need to gain the upper hand,' Vikrant said, looking worried. 'The bastards are running wild armed with assault rifles and grenades and God knows what else.'

'We're doing the usual,' Mirza said. 'Talking to their families, friends … trying to trace the van, listening to chatter…'

Vikrant sighed and closed his eyes. 'How do we smoke them out?'

'Tell me something, lad,' Mirza said. 'Which of the five Indian Mujahideen terrorists is the most attached to his family?'

Vikrant opened his eyes.

'That would be Mustafa and Ibrahim Kadir. Their mother is the only family they have, and jihad and higher purpose aside, they'd go crazy if something happened to her.'

'Something like her neighbours driving her out of her locality because they didn't want a terrorist's mother in their midst?'

'I'm pretty sure even you can't make that happen,' Vikrant told Mirza.

The older man smiled.

'I don't need to,' he said. 'I only need them to think that.'

Mirza paused. 'The chief has called for a press briefing,' he said, glancing at his watch. 'In an hour and a half.'

The veteran stood up and took out his cellphone.

'You can sedate him now,' he told the nurse as he walked out.

# 11

Hakimi wiped the sweat from his brow for the tenth time in the last minute as he walked down the aisle of the cruise liner. In spite of the cool breeze blowing off the coast of Kochi, he was feeling hot and could sense a drop of sweat threading its way from his neck down his spine, making him even more uncomfortable than he already was.

It didn't help that the muscular man with tattooed arms was standing by the railing, sipping a Diet Coke and watching the old man curiously. Hakimi, already uneasy and remembering his last encounter with the man, offered him no more than a courteous nod this time. The man, however, slowly eyed Hakimi from head to toe. Hakimi quickened his pace.

'Allah help me,' he said under his breath as he circled the deck, checked his wristwatch, wiped his forehead again and knocked on one of the cabin doors. It opened to reveal Vaishali, looking resplendent in a simple yet elegant black full-length dress and pearl choker.

'Wow!' she said as she looked at the old man, who was looking dapper in a well-fitted suit. His discomfort was evident, though, and Vaishali giggled.

'Lighten up, uncle,' she said. 'It's just a party. Look how well the suit fits you. And you didn't want to wear it!'

The owner of the cruise liner had, earlier in the day, become the proud father of a son and had ordered the captain to throw a lavish party. Vaishali had dragged Hakimi to the clothes-rental section of the cruise liner and made him select a suit, laughing as he struggled to pick the most conservative design.

'It's not just a party,' Hakimi said miserably. 'When I was growing up...'

'Uncle, I swear if you use that phrase one more time, I will tell everyone on board that it's your birthday and make you the centre of attention tonight,' Vaishali threatened.

'You wouldn't!' the old man said, horrified.

'Watch me,' she said as she took his hand and led him back through the deck. As they walked up the aisle towards the top deck, Hakimi couldn't help but cast a glance behind him. The tattooed man was no longer out there.

Determined to not let his suspicions spoil Vaishali's evening, Hakimi decided to forget about the man for the moment as they walked into the open-air party area. Whoever had organized the party knew what they were doing. One end of the deck had a bar, a small dance area, with soft lighting and slow music, while neatly dressed waiters went around with plates of snacks and drinks.

The other end, although equipped with a similar set-up, had faster, louder dance music and disco lights. The music on both ends did not clash with each other, a feat made possible by the vast expanse of deck in between, where some of the guests lounged in comfortable chairs.

As Hakimi and Vaishali settled into a couple of chairs, they were greeted by some of the other passengers with whom they had started becoming familiar.

'Looking dashing, uncle!' a teenager said as he walked past. Hakimi turned red and Vaishali laughed.

'I'm getting something to drink. What should I get you?' she asked.

'Get me one of your cocktail-type drinks,' Hakimi replied, smiling.

'That's the spirit! But non-alcoholic?' she asked. Hakimi nodded and she walked to the bar.

Hakimi took in his surroundings. A group of youngsters was grooving to some Western number he wasn't familiar with in the discotheque-like area. A few young couples nestled cozily in chairs on the deck, while a middle-aged husband and wife sat next to each other but kept eyeing the younger lot. The head waiter stood in the centre of the deck, looking completely in control, issuing orders in every direction. Hakimi had to marvel at the organized nature of the party. *They obviously run a tight ship*, he thought, chuckling at his pun.

As he looked in front, though, he stiffened. Vaishali was returning with a drink in each hand, and the man with the tattooed arms by her side. He was dressed tastefully in black trousers, a white shirt and white blazer. The top button of his shirt was undone and the blazer was left unbuttoned too.

'This is Daniel,' she said as she handed Hakimi his drink. 'Daniel, this is Abdul uncle.'

Warily, Hakimi stood up and offered his hand. 'Abdul Jabbar Hakimi,' he said, eyeing the man.

'Daniel Fernando,' the man said, taking his hand in a firm grip.

A hundred nautical miles away, Marco, dressed in black combat fatigues, slipped a stiletto dagger in the holster around his right ankle. His Uzi was hanging by its strap and his Glock was snug in his thigh holster as he slid down the rope ladder to the dinghy, checking his utility belt, which had spare ammo clips in its pouches.

His fellow soldiers, similarly outfitted, were already on the dinghy. Marco turned around to take one last look at Marwan, who was standing on the deck. Marco offered a wave. Marwan responded with a thumbs-up.

Marco lit a cigarette and nodded to his second in command, Omar, who fired up the motor.

# 12

Shahwaz Ali Mirza was tired. It was 11.30 in the night and he had been in the Mumbai office of the NIA since the previous afternoon, having gone there straight from the hospital after his chat with Vikrant. On the way, he had made a series of quick calls and then called his boss, NIA chief T. Rangaswamy, fifteen minutes before the latter was to begin his press briefing.

Rangaswamy had only listened, with the occasional 'Hmm' thrown in every now and then, and then said, 'You're sure about this?'

'No, sir. But frankly, we're doing everything we can,' Mirza had replied. Rangaswamy replied that he understood.

And so it was that half an hour later, during the press briefing, a reporter who had managed to raise his voice above the others' asked, 'Sir, our colleagues in Mumbai tell us that the mother of two of the five terrorists was driven out of her house by her neighbours. What do you know about that?'

Rangaswamy had hesitated for just the right number of seconds before saying, 'I think the Mumbai police will be in a better position to comment on that.'

It was beautifully done, Mirza thought later. His boss had not confirmed it but not denied it either, and the pause had worked well to further stoke curiosity and suspicion. Mirza had called up the Mumbai cops who had quietly planted the seed among their reporter friends. Next, he had texted Rangaswamy, thanking him, who had replied with a '☺'.

An hour earlier, a team of female constables in plainclothes had quietly picked up Mustafa and Ibrahim Kadir's mother, Shagufta Bi, from her residence in Behrambaug and taken her to the Crime Branch headquarters, where the bewildered old woman was made comfortable in a spare office, given food and drink and told that 'bade sahab' would see her soon.

In the meantime, Mirza had discreetly planted his operatives around her house, and also placed Shagufta Bi's cellphone, as well as the phones of all her neighbours and family members, under surveillance.

Then the waiting began. Through the evening, Mirza spoke to his family in Delhi, checked on the health of his men in the hospital, made calls to his friends in RAW and IB, touched base with his informants and paced about the NIA office in Mumbai where the surveillance was being monitored. And still there were no results.

When results did come, it was from somewhere unexpected. Mirza was stretched out on a couch in the office lobby to rest his aching back when his cellphone buzzed. The voice was not too familiar and it took him a moment to realize that it was the superintendent of police, Palghar, who, after the shootout, had been personally supervising a search for the terrorists.

'We may have found something, sir,' the SP said.

'Keep talking,' Mirza said, picking himself up.

'There's a van on fire some distance away from the main road, in the forest area, on the outskirts of Palghar district,' she replied.

'White with sliding doors?' Mirza asked hopefully.

'Yes, and I think I see some dents in the doors. It is difficult to make out as it's still burning, but I think they are dents made by pistol rounds, sir. The fire brigade just got here.'

Mirza jumped off the couch.

'Do not use water. Do you hear? Tell the fire brigade to not use water. Use the other damn thing but not a drop of water!' he roared.

It took Mirza close to two hours to get from the NIA office to the spot in Palghar where the van had been found, and by this time, the fire brigade had put out the blaze using foam and was spraying coolant on the van so that it could be examined at the earliest. Cursorily returning the SP's salute, Mirza barged ahead and accosted the first fire officer he could see.

'How much longer?' he demanded.

The exhausted and soot-laden officer turned to snap at the impudent man but checked himself when he saw the SP standing respectfully behind Mirza.

'Not much longer, sir. Ten more minutes.'

'Thanks, man. And great work,' Mirza said, patting the fireman's arm and earning a tired smile before turning to the team of forensic experts he had picked up on the way from the Forensic Sciences Laboratory in Kalina.

'You people ready?' he asked. They were already snapping their gloves on. 'Move in the minute he says you can,' he added and pulled out his cellphone, which was buzzing. It was Vikrant, calling to ask for an update, and he could hear the nurse protesting behind him.

'Hang tight, lad,' he told his protégé and hung up.

For the next hour, Mirza examined every little piece pulled out by the forensic experts, either discarding it as rubbish or adding it to the pile of possible clues. Spent shells and a couple of empty ammunition clips went in a large plastic bag and one of the lab guys left immediately to run ballistics tests on them. Every little shred of paper was carefully put into plastic bags and filed away. A separate team of experts would go over them later.

The team was nearing the end of its search when one of the experts picked up a small cloth pouch from under the rear passenger seat. Digging between the seat and the backrest, he came up with a piece of paper around eight inches long and five inches wide, torn in an irregular pattern and singed at the edges, but largely intact.

Curiously, Mirza took the paper from him and examined it under the light of a torch.

For several minutes, he stared intently at it. Then he ran the torchlight up and down the paper for another three minutes before he looked up.

'Bloody hell,' he said, wide-eyed and breathing heavily. 'Bloody fucking hell!'

# 13

*Wednesday morning, cruise liner.*

The sunlight streaming in through the porthole of her room woke up Vaishali. She turned away from it, burying her face in Daniel's bare chest. He put his arm around her and snuggled closer. Vaishali purred like a kitten, making him laugh softly.

'Don't laugh, rascal,' she said sleepily, looking up and kissing his chin. 'I'm going to be sore all over for the next week.'

She still didn't know exactly why she had invited him to join her and Hakimi the previous night, when she had seen him sitting at the bar by himself, but she was glad she did. The party went on till late into the night and throughout, she had sensed Hakimi throwing looks of disapproval towards her as she got more and more comfortable with Daniel. Even the conversation between the two men had been strained. While Daniel was reserved but polite, Hakimi was wary and clipped.

As soon as Daniel had gone to get another round of drinks for them, Hakimi glared at Vaishali. 'What are you doing!' he asked in a hushed voice.

'What?' she asked, startled.

'That man is bad news.'

She looked puzzled.

'I just ... don't have a very good feeling about him,' Hakimi said.

Vaishali giggled. 'That's the man you were telling me about, isn't it?' she asked. 'The one who didn't laugh at your joke?'

'That's got nothing to do with it,' Hakimi said, glaring.

Before they could argue over it, Daniel returned with their drinks. Hakimi, after finishing his, excused himself.

'Old men like me can't party like you lot,' he said with a polite smile and retired to his room.

Daniel and Vaishali had talked till late into the night, discussing everything under the sun from politics to pasta recipes, and while she found Daniel to be guarded when it came to his personal life, he was also knowledgeable and well-travelled. On the same whim that had prompted her to invite him, she had asked if he would like to walk her to her room.

'Wouldn't be much of a gentleman if I didn't, would I?' he said with a small smile.

'Isn't this the wrong era for chivalry?' she countered.

'It's never the wrong era for chivalry,' he assured her, offering his hand. She put hers in his, stood up and they walked hand in hand till they reached her room. That was when she'd realized she didn't want to let go.

Turning to face him, she'd looked into his eyes and for the first time seen a deep sadness hidden just behind the surface, similar to the one she carried within her. Without thinking, she put her other arm around his neck and felt him slip his arm around her waist. They kissed, gently at first and then, as they both grew surer of themselves, with reckless abandon. The rest of the night was a hazy memory of mad, rough lovemaking that had left them both exhausted. They went to sleep in each other's arms at dawn.

'Oh, you're gonna be sore? I've got love bites all over my neck. Good thing I packed a couple of turtlenecks,' Daniel now said, gently slapping Vaishali's buttocks as she laughed.

'I wonder what Abdul uncle will say,' she said suddenly.

'You should tell him just to see his reaction.' Daniel laughed.

Vaishali drew herself up on her elbow and looked at Daniel as he turned and rested on his back.

'I think I'll tell him. Just to piss him off,' he said, earning a gentle slap.

'What is it with you two?' she asked curiously.

Daniel shrugged. 'He tried to chat me up on a day when I was in an extremely bad mood. The next time I saw him, he was all dolled up in that suit, looking supremely uncomfortable, and I was afraid I'd start laughing if I tried to say anything.'

'You're so awful! He wasn't dolled up!'

'But he was looking utterly uncomfortable.'

'He was looking cute.'

'Fine. I'll pull his cheeks when I see him today,' Daniel said, getting off the bed. Vaishali slapped his ass.

'You're really into slapping, aren't you? And I don't mean only this morning,' he said, looking at her with a smirk as she blushed furiously, hiding her face in the pillow. He went to take a shower. She looked up from the pillow, thought for a second and then went in after him.

Forty-five minutes later, they were both walking across the deck, Vaishali in a simple t-shirt and jeans, and Daniel in the previous night's rumpled clothes.

'I'll change and join you for breakfast,' he said as they reached his room, kissing her on the lips and sending her on her way with a light slap on her behind.

'Rascal,' she muttered as she went to the cafeteria on the top deck.

Daniel entered his room and undressed quickly. Despite the shower, having to put on last night's clothes had made him uncomfortable and he took a second quick shower before slipping on a pair of cargoes and a t-shirt. Just then his cellphone buzzed with a text message.

'Found myself missing you again last night. It really hurts to not have you,' it read.

He stared at the phone for a second, resisting the impulse to smash it on the floor. Taking a deep breath, he told himself that after a long time, he was feeling something resembling happiness and was not going to let this message ruin it.

'Wish you'd thought of that before you cheated on me. Also, I'm blocking your number. Bye,' he replied.

After six months of promising to do so, he actually did put the number in the block list and smiled at the enormous sense of peace it gave him. He'd call his service provider today itself and get them to block it permanently.

Still smiling, Daniel walked out of his room, feeling better than he had in ages and made his way up to the cafeteria, looking forward to seeing Vaishali again. He'd apologize to Hakimi and start afresh with him too, he decided.

He came up to the top deck and stopped in his tracks. Vaishali, Hakimi and several other guests, along with the captain and the entire crew, were sitting on the ground outside the cafeteria, their hands behind their heads. Behind them, several dark-complexioned men in black fatigues stood with Uzis in their hands. Somalis or Nigerians, he guessed. As his survival instinct kicked in, he felt his fingers curl into fists. At that instant, something jabbed him in his right side. He glanced down to see the barrel of an Uzi against his ribs and up again into the smiling face of a stocky, muscular black man.

'Name's Marco, friend,' he said. 'And as of right now, I be the captain of this little ship.'

# 14

Vikrant had a headache and it had nothing to do with his recent injuries.

At the crack of dawn he had been woken up by Mirza, who looked like he had a fishbone stuck in his throat. Almost whispering, he asked Vikrant if he could walk and the younger cop nodded. Mirza waited till Vikrant struggled off the bed and slipped on a pair of slippers, then left the room quietly, gesturing to Vikrant to follow him. Vikrant slowly limped behind.

As the two of them made their way to the terrace, Vikrant's curiosity rose with each second. The two men came to a stop in a corner of the terrace and Mirza finally spoke.

'What do you know about the '93 Cache?' he asked.

'I'm fairly sure it's not the next Frederick Forsyth novel. Or an upcoming Ridley Scott movie,' Vikrant said, leaning against a wall.

Mirza didn't smile. Vikrant turned serious.

'What's wrong?' he asked.

Mirza sighed.

'In 1993, the ISI sent firepower by the crates to Tiger Memon, which was received at Shekhadi in Konkan. Some of it was RDX, which was used to create IEDs that were planted all over Mumbai city, leading to the serial blasts. The rest of it comprised AK-56 assault rifles, fresh off the assembly lines from Pakistani arms' factories.'

Vikrant nodded and waited for Mirza to go on. He already knew this part.

'Well, the officers who interrogated the arrested at the time had a theory, one which has since then been passed down the generations. According to this, some part of the arsenal was never used. It was hidden away safely in multiple locations known only to the ISI and those close to them, to be used at a later date. Many of us believe that it is lying ready to be used for another terrorist attack on the city, particularly the assault rifles.'

Mirza stopped and turned to Vikrant, who was staring at him wide-eyed.

'And that's the '93 Cache?' the protégé asked.

'That is the '93 Cache.'

'Why don't I know about this?' Vikrant wondered aloud.

Mirza shrugged.

'You do now.'

'Why *didn't* I know about this?' Vikrant snapped.

'It's a theory, kid. There's been no evidence to support it. Only whispers from here and there, time and again. Some say the old timers who are still in jail for the '93 blasts case know the locations and will take the knowledge to their graves. Others say that some of them have revealed the location to their sons, nephews and such. A wilder theory is that someone prepared a map which is regularly passed around among the sleeper cells in Mumbai and Thane,' Mirza explained.

It was at this point that Vikrant's head began to ache.

'Give me the bad news already,' he said, sighing.

Mirza reached into his shirt pocket, pulled out a folded sheet of paper and handed it over. Vikrant unfolded it and held it against the light on the terrace. It was an enlarged colour photocopy of the piece of paper that the forensic technicians had salvaged from the burnt-out van three hours ago.

'Forensics pulled this out of the van at Palghar,' Mirza said.

It looked like the top half of a page from a logbook, torn in a way that suggested that it had happened in a hurry or by accident. It contained two lines of text followed by two entries, one under the other, separated by two blank lines. Both the entries were bullet points written in Urdu.

Vikrant, at Mirza's suggestion, had taken up learning to read and write Urdu two years earlier, and hence, he could easily read the entries.

*'There is no God but Allah, and Mohammad is His Prophet.*

*May this material aid you in your noble quest as it has others before you.*

*Sativli. Shafiq. Nephew of Raza. Green cottage. Brooms. Grains.*

*Narpoli. Anwar. Son of Aslam. Second floor. Blue
building by the park. Soap.'*

'Soap,' Vikrant said.

'Yes,' Mirza replied.

RDX is informally referred to as sabun or soap in Hindi. The
ISI agents who had trained Indian Muslims in the assembling
and handling of IEDs in 1993 would refer to RDX as 'kaala
sabun' or black soap.

Vikrant looked at Mirza.

'At least it's not a map,' he said to diffuse the tension. His
mentor shot him a look of irritation.

'What do you think?' Mirza asked.

Vikrant took half a minute before he spoke.

'It's a list maintained and updated with each passing year. If
this is about the '93 Cache, and I'm still hoping to God it isn't,
it means that the arsenal is being passed down from father to
son, or uncle to nephew, and its locations and identities of the
current caretakers are being updated.'

Vikrant paused and looked at the image again.

'This, for example, could have been made any time between
the last ten days to ten years. And if soap stands for RDX, I'd
say brooms are AK-56 assault rifles and grains are ammunition
rounds. The vague addresses are obviously a precaution, in case
the list falls into wrong hands,' Vikrant finished.

Mirza nodded.

'We have teams scouring for the green cottage in Sativli and
the blue building in Nashik Camp,' he said. 'But I doubt whether

finding them is going to be of much use. What concerns me is what might be on the rest of that list.'

'As well as how long the list is. And what it contains, aside from soap, brooms and grains,' said Vikrant.

'At least now we know where the fuckers got the AKs from,' Mirza said.

'We also know that they, in all probability, have RDX too.'

Both men silently pondered over the implications of what they had just discussed.

# 15

The rest of the morning saw the same scene being played out on loop – the guests would come up to the cafeteria for breakfast, stop at the sight of their fellow passengers being held at gunpoint and then join their ranks. Those who called for room service were told by the head waiter, who had a gun to his head, that due to some issues breakfast would be served only in the cafeteria. The gunmen took away the guests' cellphones and subjected each one to a body search, including the women, before making them sit on the floor in the middle of the top deck.

This continued for about two hours. All the while, Omar kept count and finally nodded to Marco.

'Okay!' Marco said jovially. 'We have thirty guests up here now. That's all of them, right, captain?' he asked the captain of the ship, who only nodded. Omar dragged him to where Marco was standing.

Marco's face hardened for a minute as he said, 'You lie to me, I shoot one of your guests. Clear?'

Captain Rajeshwar Sahani looked into Marco's eye, saw that he meant business and nodded.

'Good. How many crew?'

'Seven,' Sahani said.

'How many staff?'

'Ten.'

Marco turned Sahani around so that he was facing the captives.

'Anyone missing?' Marco asked.

Sahani took his time before shaking his head.

'The count adds up,' he said.

Marco nodded, as if in approval of Sahani's compliance, and ordered four of his men to search the cruise liner.

'If they return with a single person they find hidin' in some corner, one of the passengers dies,' he told Sahani before turning to the guests.

'People,' he said, 'no need to worry. You do as we say, we treat you with love and care. But you do somethin' I don't like, bodies start fallin'. So, help us to help you, eh?'

Marco was smiling as he turned back to the captain.

'How d' you communicate with land?' he asked.

'Radio,' Sahani replied.

'Show me,' Marco said.

He marched Marco down to the engine room, passing one of his soldiers on the way, who reported that he did not find anyone hiding.

In the engine room, Sahani led Marco to the radio. Marco took a good long look around the room and then marched Sahani back to the top deck. Omar was perched casually atop a table in the cafeteria, Uzi resting against his thigh, chatting with the head waiter.

'Food twice a day for everyone. Water as per need. No alcoholic drinks. Liquor creates heroes and we don't need no heroes, right?' Omar was saying.

The head waiter, numb with fear, could only nod.

Marco led Sahani to where the others were sitting and pushed him down among them.

'Like you must have observed,' Marco said, raising his voice, 'my men are makin' sure you all be comfortable. So respect our efforts and don't do nothin' stupid. We'll get in touch with your government and soon y'all be sittin' with your folks back home, tellin' stories of how you got hijacked and shit.'

The other Somalis had by now searched the liner and come back up.

'All clear?' Marco asked them and they responded in the affirmative.

'All right. Take positions,' he said.

Ten of his men headed downstairs, while Marco and Omar remained where they were. Five minutes later, Marco's earpiece crackled. He acknowledged the report and turned to the captives.

'On your feet!' he ordered, his amiable facade slipping away in a second, jolting everyone.

Omar stepped forward.

'Get in a single line and walk,' he told the captives in his gruff voice. 'Start!'.

The passengers did as they were told, marching down to the second level, heads down. Marco's men were spread out evenly along the way, guns ready, eyes alert. Only Daniel surreptitiously took stock of each man as he passed by him, taking in his build, stance, weapons and every other detail.

The second level of the cruise liner had the engine room at one end, and a large recreational area spanning the rest of the floor, where the hostages were led. The shutters on the windows had been drawn by the time they entered the area, where they were made to sit again.

'We'll leave y'all on your own now. But no tricks, please. My men will be standing outside each door. You stick a finger out without permission, it will be shot off. Your head will be next,' Marco said before walking out, followed by Omar and the rest of his gang.

Both the doors to the recreation hall slid shut. And then there was silence.

For nearly ten minutes, no one spoke. Then Hakimi cleared his throat and everyone turned to him.

'I have a friend in the maritime trade business,' Hakimi began. 'He tells me that ships of all kinds, be it commercial, trade or cruise liners like ours, are frequently hijacked by Somali pirates and held to ransom.'

A few people nodded their heads, murmuring their agreement.

'What we need to bear in mind,' Hakimi went on, 'is that every vessel is insured and the owners do not hesitate in paying up whatever the pirates demand. There is also a government authority that helps with the negotiations. I forget the name...'

'Directorate general of shipping,' said Daniel and everyone now turned to him.

Hakimi nodded. 'That's right, young man. The DG, shipping. So there is really no cause for worry. The pirates have displayed no signs of wanting to harm us as long as we do not give them reason to do so,' he said with a reassuring smile.

'Except they're not pirates,' Daniel said.

Once again, everyone turned their gaze from Hakimi to Daniel. Hakimi glared a little.

'I'm trying to keep up the morale here, Mr Fernando. So if you're going to be pessimistic...'

'I'm not being pessimistic. And morale based on false hopes does more damage when shattered,' Daniel replied.

'Maybe ... maybe you should tell us why you think they're not pirates, Dan,' Vaishali spoke up.

'Somali pirates hijack vessels because they need food and other stuff for their people back home. They're usually skinny, though not weak, and are armed with AK-47s, which are far easier to acquire in the illegal weapons market. Their idea of hijacking a vessel is to storm aboard, take over all supplies, wrangle whatever more they can from the owner and get the hell out,' Daniel said.

'O... okay...' Vaishali said, trying to wrap her head around it.

'These men are well-built and obviously able to plan and strategize. They sneaked aboard in the dead of night and had the crew in control by the time we woke up. And remember, we were partying till late in the night. Who was the last to leave?' Daniel asked.

A boy in his twenties raised his hand hesitantly. 'Me and my friends were pretty wasted but we're sure there was no one around by the time we left at, say, 4 in the morning,' he said.

'And who was the first to get up there this morning?'

'That would be me,' Hakimi said. 'I'm an early riser and I reached the cafeteria around 7 o'clock.'

'Which means,' Daniel said, 'that in three hours, they boarded, went to the engine room, subdued the captain and his crew, took them up to the top deck and overpowered the staff as well. Not to mention they've got Uzis, sophisticated Israeli sub-machine guns, plus Glock automatic pistols, another gun of superior quality as well as daggers in their boots. And the way they move and stand indicates that they have been in combat before. Proper battlefield combat.'

'I'm sure you're just making that last one up,' a middle-aged woman said. 'How can you guess that from their movement and stance?'

'Because that's exactly how I move and stand,' said Daniel. 'As do all the others who were in the army with me.'

# 16

The session that had begun at 11 a.m. in the doctor's office at the Kokilaben Ambani Hospital showed no signs of getting over anytime soon.

Mirza, DCP Ashok Mankame and DSPs Samar Goyal and Akhil Jaiswal were sitting on chairs while Vikrant was sprawled out on a couch against a pillow, head thrown back, eyes closed. Vikrant often sat that way, in what Mirza called his 'samadhi' position, during brainstorming sessions with his colleagues.

Jaiswal had a brace around his neck, while the others were adorned with bandages of all shapes and sizes. The exceptions were Mirza, whose injuries were nothing more than scars by now, and Mankame, whose ankle had healed.

'Okay, lads. First things first,' Mirza said. 'We found a green cottage around two kilometres from the site of the shootout in

73

Sativli, belonging to one Shafiq Attarwala. He used to stay there with his family.'

'Used to?' Vikrant asked.

'He's not been seen or heard from since the day of the shootout. There's more. We searched his house. There was a trunk in one of the bedrooms, big enough to hold AK-56 assault rifles. And ammo could have been stored anywhere.'

Several curses were muttered before Mirza went on.

'We also found a blue-painted residential building across the street from a public park in Narpoli, Bhiwandi. A guy named Anwar, a tailor by profession, used to stay with his wife and three kids on the second floor. All are missing since yesterday. The house looked like he'd packed and left in a hurry. And our teams found three airtight plastic containers strewn in his bedroom.'

'Soap,' Vikrant said morosely.

'Bloody hope not,' said Mankame.

'Right,' Mirza continued. 'Let's move on. You've all seen the document. What do you think?'

After half a minute's silence, Goyal spoke up. 'Well, sir, don't the clues seem too obvious? I mean, anyone could have found those two houses...'

'Only if they had that list,' Vikrant interrupted. 'The real feat would have been to get the list in the first place, and it would not be given to any Tom, Dick or Hafeez.'

'Plus, if I'm not wrong,' Mankame chipped in, 'the clues needed to be obvious, right, sir? I mean, terrorists are brutal and ruthless and all that, but how many do we know who are actually smart?'

Mirza nodded in approval.

'Why now?' Jaiswal asked and everyone turned to him, except for Vikrant. 'If they've had the cache since 1993, why wait all these years to use it? The city was much more vulnerable earlier. But after 26/11, we've beefed up the security like anything. We have the Force One, an NSG hub here, CCTV cameras, coastal security and even our intelligence network is better than what it used to be.'

'All of which is aimed at preventing another 26/11, that is, an attack from outside, not within. Imagine if you only had to hand the list to five men and let them do their job. They even grew up in Mumbai and know the city well. You don't even have to smuggle anyone into the city,' Mirza countered.

'Time is also a factor,' Vikrant said and everyone turned to him. Without opening his eyes, he continued, 'Intelligence sources had been hearing about the '93 Cache for twenty-three years but not seeing a single sign of it. Over time, they began to think it was just a wild theory and as the years passed, they started giving it such little importance that Mirza sir didn't even think of mentioning it to me.'

Mankame nodded and took it up. 'Had we not found the piece of paper, we would still be in the dark about the cache and those motherfuckers would have killed us in our sleep. We can get all the infrastructure we can afford but this complacence is what is going to end our existence one day.'

Vikrant half-turned to his counterpart, opened one eye and acknowledged his contribution with a nod before resuming his samadhi position.

'It also shows enormous patience, the patience of a hunter. And the ISI is fully capable of that,' Mirza added.

After a minute's silence, Mankame spoke up again.

'Sir, you said that they, as in the ISI, just needed to send five men to pick up the arms and execute the attack. What I can't help wondering is, why these five? More so, why break them out of jail when they could have sent any of their trained operatives for the job?' Mankame wondered.

'Maybe because they already had the list when they were arrested,' Vikrant said, now slowly easing himself into a sitting position.

'I have no way to know for sure, but I arrested these fuckers,' he went on. 'And I interrogated them for days. They had gone to Bhopal to steal vehicles. Can you believe that? Mumbai to Bhopal, just for that? Again, enormous patience and planning. We seized seven stolen cars from them later. But not a single weapon. Not even a country-made gun or a dagger.'

'So what are you saying, son?' Mirza asked.

'Well, in their interrogation, we kept asking them about weapons and they kept claiming they were innocent. In fact, had it not been for all the writings on jihad and photographs of sensitive installations we found on them, we'd have had to book them for nothing more than vehicle theft. Now it makes sense.'

Mirza nodded slowly. 'A list leading to the '93 Cache. That's a secret worth dying for,' he said.

'More than that,' Vikrant reasoned. 'If Shaukat Asad had the only copy of the list – and I'd like to believe that the ISI is not as stupid as to make multiple copies – it was the best insurance he had. Once the list was passed on to someone else, the ISI would simply wash their hands off him and his men, or even have them killed.'

'And that,' Mirza said, 'is why they were broken out.'

Mankame, Jaiswal and Goyal silently watched as protégé and mentor unravelled the threads of the web. It was as if only the two of them were in the room at the moment.

'Fuck,' Vikrant breathed. 'That is what Asad's uncle went to fetch from his father in Cheetah Camp ... Didn't Forensics find a pouch?'

'Yup.'

'We need to show it to Shakeel Khan and see if he will identify it.'

'But then, boy, this means...'

'This means that Asad – or someone else from that module – got hold of the list and left it at his house for safekeeping while they scoped out targets and arranged for vehicles. They were going to retrieve the list and get the arsenal in the end, because who would want to carry the list around while everything else was being put in place? But then they got busted,' said Vikrant.

'And someone reached out to them while they were in jail. Someone who told them that they only had to break out on their own and all the help they needed would be provided. Which is how they had vehicles waiting for them. And weapons. They just needed to get the list,' Mirza replied.

'But,' Goyal interrupted, 'they were already in Sativli, where the first location was. How did they know they had to start there?'

Vikrant shrugged. 'If they had had something as legendary as the '93 Cache list, they would have read it over and over. The first item on the list is the least anyone would remember. But they would need the entire list to complete their mission. It's not conclusive, but it fits in with basic human behaviour.'

Everyone nodded.

'Which means,' Mirza said, looking at Vikrant, 'they collected the weapons from Sativli, took the list from Khan, then went to Bhiwandi. They tore off the top part of the list after memorizing second location and it was supposed to have burned with the van.'

'The list is being destroyed. Because it will no longer be needed,' Vikrant said.

There was a minute's silence as everyone in the room digested this.

'I'm telling the PMO,' Mirza announced.

# 17

Daniel went up to the door of the recreation hall and knocked on it. He had to knock thrice before it was opened by a surly-faced Somali with a cigarette dangling from his mouth.

'What?' the guard asked.

'That,' Daniel said, pointing to the cigarette.

The other man raised an eyebrow.

'Many of us are smokers,' Daniel said calmly. 'And it's been hours since we last had a smoke. We'd like our cigarettes and lighters. Some of us were carrying them, but most left them in our rooms.'

'I ain't runnin' a fuckin' five-star hotel,' the Somali snarled. 'You people are hostages, in case it ain't clear.'

Daniel nodded.

'But even hostages have their vices, and nicotine withdrawal causes some very unpleasant symptoms. I'm sure you guys want us all to be docile and obedient, and a little nicotine will

79

go a long way in ensuring that,' he said, keeping his voice low and polite.

The guard continued staring at Daniel for several tense moments, and right when everyone thought he was going to shoot Daniel in the face, the hijacker shut the door.

Daniel turned around, smiling.

'That went well,' one of his fellow captives said.

'Wait,' Daniel told him as he went back to sit on the floor next to Vaishali.

They waited for over twenty-five minutes before the door opened again and Marco sauntered in, followed by his surly-faced soldier, who was carrying a plastic bag.

'Which one of you asked for cigarettes?' Marco said pleasantly and everyone stiffened, except for Daniel, who stood up.

'That'd be me, sir,' he said.

Daniel and Marco looked at each other for a long moment before Marco, without breaking eye contact, signalled his surly subordinate. The latter stepped forward and dropped the bag on the floor, after which he walked out of the room.

'Step forward, would you, mister?' Marco said to Daniel and both men walked towards each other, meeting halfway.

'You can play union leader all day long if it helps you pass the time,' Marco told him. 'Just don't forget who's really in charge here.'

'Of course not, sir,' Daniel said, giving Marco a small smile.

'We rounded up all the cigarettes we could find in the rooms,' Marco continued.

'Thanks a lot,' Daniel responded.

'Anything else? Chocolates? Ice cream?'

'Could you tell us about the status of the negotiations with our government?'

'Goin' on. They have our demands and are playin' their usual games.'

Daniel nodded.

'Thank you, sir,' he said.

Marco turned around and walked out, closing the door.

Daniel waited for several seconds before saying, 'He's lying.'

'What?' Hakimi asked, looking sour. He had vehemently opposed Daniel's idea of asking for cigarettes, saying that their captors should not be antagonized in any way. He had lost to the sheer number of smokers in the room.

Coolly, Daniel walked over to the carry bag, fished out a packet of cigarettes and took one.

'He's not contacted our government,' he said, rummaging inside the bag for a lighter.

'How do you know?' Vaishali asked.

'Because I know a liar when I see one,' Daniel said, and Hakimi scoffed.

'Also,' Daniel went on. 'Proof of life.'

'I was thinking the same thing.' Captain Rajeshwar Sahani spoke up. All eyes turned to him.

'If they had contacted our government,' he went on, 'the first thing they would have asked for is proof that we're alive and unhurt. These men would have made one of us speak to someone, or taken a picture or a video or something. Negotiations wouldn't have gone ahead unless our government had confirmation of our well-being. Also, they're making the crew maintain contact with the head office, pretending that everything is fine.'

Daniel gave the captain a sharp look. 'They are?' he asked.

Sahani nodded. 'I've been asked to stay on the course mapped out for the cruise and take all the halts as scheduled.'

'Why is that significant?' Hakimi asked, interested in spite of himself.

'Because,' Daniel said, puffing away at his cigarette, 'if they were really pirates, they would already be talking to the DG, Shipping, by now. That would have been the first thing they would have done as soon as they had us all under control. Instead, they're planning meals twice a day and giving us cigarettes to keep us happy.'

'It's as if they don't want their presence found out just yet,' Sahani added.

'Planning and forethought,' Daniel said.

'So, why are they lying?' someone asked.

'My guess? They're waiting.'

'For what?' Vaishali asked.

'Orders,' Daniel said. 'Marco can claim to be running the show all he wants. But he's taking orders from someone else.'

# 18

The news about the '93 Cache exploded in the offices of various government establishments like a bomb, as Mirza had expected. The Prime Minister's Office gave the clichéd politician's response, ordering Mirza to sweep it under the carpet.

'Why spread panic when we're not even sure?' was the official line. The veteran spy, well versed with the nature of politics, simply smiled, nodded and walked out.

'That went well,' NIA chief T. Rangaswamy, who had accompanied Mirza to the PMO, said while they were on their way back to the NIA headquarters in Delhi.

'Exactly as we'd expected it to,' Mirza responded.

'Plan B?' Rangaswamy asked.

Plan B was to step up vigilance in Maharashtra, particularly in Mumbai, but quietly. The same day, Rangaswamy had a discreet meeting with the head of the Intelligence Bureau, in

Amritsar at his behest, apprising the latter of the situation, including the PMO's reaction. The IB chief listened without taking any notes and nodded in understanding. He was known to be a man of few words and, having worked with Mirza earlier, knew better than to doubt his inputs.

Mirza, meanwhile, flew back to Mumbai and had a meeting with the DGP, Maharashtra, and the Mumbai police commissioner the next day. After some effort, he managed to convince both of them that there was a good chance the '93 Cache really existed.

'How do we know it's not a smokescreen?' DGP Paramjeet Kalra asked, and Mirza had to stop himself from snapping, 'You think we didn't think of that already? For fuck's sake!' But he was, in spite of his enviable field experience as a spy, only an IG-rank officer, while the other two were his seniors. Instead, he said, 'I don't think so, sir. It's too elaborate a smokescreen to be thought up by five IM recruits, even if they're acting for the ISI. In fact, very few in the ISI are capable of such detailed planning.'

'Besides,' Mumbai CP Virendra Sinha spoke up, 'if this is a smokescreen, what are they actually planning? Something even bigger and more elaborate? Too improbable, sir.'

Kalra sighed. 'Do what you have to do, but do it quietly,' he said.

And with that, Maharashtra went into high-alert mode. Additional police cover was provided to sensitive installations, airports and railway stations, without making it too obvious. VIP security was stepped up. Traffic police would stop and search any suspicious-looking vehicle at all hours. Police personnel visited all the hotels and lodges within their jurisdictions and verified the credentials of recent check-ins. On-ground intelligence gathering was stepped up as well, especially in slum pockets where one could rent a room and pay in cash without any questions asked. Crime Branch officers picked up former convicts of all kinds and badgered them for fresh tip-offs. Raids were conducted at godowns, warehouses, commercial freighters and anywhere else the '93 Cache could be hidden.

The IB put pressure on all its sources to find out the tiniest whisper about any mysterious activity in and around Maharashtra. The internet was scanned every day and phones of suspected miscreants were intercepted to pick up any chatter. Rangaswamy was in touch with the IB chief on a daily basis. Both Mirza and he spoke to their friends in Western intelligence agencies hoping that something as big as the '93 Cache would generate at least some buzz in the global Islamic terrorist network.

Vikrant was officially still under suspension, only a 'consultant' on the Bhopal jailbreak case. He spent his days cooped up in the NIA office. But he was busy collaborating with the Maharashtra Anti-Terrorism Squad, his old posting, speaking to the ATS chief twice a day and providing his inputs on where the ATS should be looking next.

After five days of intense effort, Rangaswamy, Mirza and Vikrant all had to agree on one thing – the five Indian Mujahideen members seemed to have vanished without a trace.

On the evening of the seventh day, Vikrant, followed by Goyal, Jaiswal and Mankame, entered the cabin that Mirza had taken over in the Mumbai NIA office. Vikrant sat himself on a chair in front of Mirza, who was leafing through a report, and placed a thick stack of papers on the desk.

'Unless those are Google Earth printouts showing the locations of the IM Five,' Mirza said irascibly, 'I'm not interested.'

Vikrant shook his head.

'I think we've pretty much realized that this case isn't moving forward anymore. Rather, we're just moving in circles,' he said.

'You have a better idea?' his mentor snapped.

Vikrant nodded and tapped the stack of papers.

'How about we go backwards?' he asked.

# 19

*Thursday morning, one week later, cruise liner.*

'Why did you quit the army?' Vaishali asked, resting her head against Daniel's shoulder.

'My father,' Daniel replied, flicking a few strands of hair off her face. 'He was the only family I ever had, and his health had already deteriorated a lot by the time I realized that he wasn't getting any younger. I took voluntary retirement four years ago and did all I could for him till his death.'

Daniel and Vaishali were nestled against each other in one corner of the recreational area. Over the last seven days, the hostages had sorted themselves into groups. Families with children had gravitated towards each other, while the youngsters had formed a group of their own. Hakimi had joined a motley group of men of all ages, while Daniel and Vaishali, tired of hiding their feelings for each other after the second day, stuck to each other. Captain Sahani kept going around the space, talking to everyone and making sure they were all right. His crew members were imprisoned in the engine room. Before he was separated from them, Sahani had told them to just do what they were told and not do anything stupid.

Daniel's mention of his father's death made Vaishali look up at him.

'I'm sorry,' she said. 'I know what it's like.'

Daniel nodded. 'You told me. Your mother.'

They reached out at the same time and took each other's hand.

'It doesn't hurt?' she asked. 'To talk about it?'

'A lot of things hurt. Doesn't mean I have to let it show every time.'

'And I thought I was damaged,' she mused.

'Aren't we all?' he said, looking around him out of habit.

By now the hostages had settled into a routine. Their captors – who seemed to be mercenaries of some kind, according to Daniel – would lead the kitchen crew up to the cafeteria every morning to prepare sandwiches and milkshakes for everyone. The meals were served thrice a day and never varied. The recreational area had two large washrooms, which took care of daily ablutions and toilet visits.

Every morning, Marco would lead Sahani to the radio room so that he could maintain regular contact with his colleagues back in Mumbai, and take him and the kitchen crew back to the recreational area at night. Sahani would interact with his crew every time he went there. They were all being treated well but watched closely.

However, the hostages were getting restless. They had not changed their clothes in seven days, and Marco had refused to allow anyone access to razors or scissors, so all the men had stubbles by now. Almost everyone was irritated at having to wear the same soiled clothes every day after taking a wash. Only Daniel, who had seen worse, remained calm.

'It's a control tactic,' he explained to Vaishali when she wondered why they weren't even being given fresh clothes. 'Allow them to get too comfortable and they might turn mutinous. Keep them fed and give them basic facilities, but at the same time, deny them more than is strictly necessary. It helps keep them obedient.'

'What are you so relaxed about?' Vaishali asked.

Daniel smiled.

'I know they're not simple pirates. And they don't know that I do. Every step they take to mislead us into believing they're pirates is actually a peep into their actual plan. And when the time comes, that knowledge will help me.'

'When the time comes?' Vaishali wondered.

'What, you think I'm letting us die here?' he said.

'Damn it, Dan. You can't take on ten armed men by yourself, no matter what commando stuff you did back in the army,' she whispered, alarmed.

'There are twelve of them,' he corrected. 'And they're giving me a lot of time to plan while they wait for their orders.'

Vaishali squeezed his hand.

'Let's talk about something else,' Daniel said, caressing her hair.

She nodded. 'Like what?' she asked.

'Like your Abdul uncle glaring at me every time he sees me within five metres of you, which, frankly, is all the time,' Daniel said, grinning.

It worked. Vaishali smiled and slapped his thigh lightly.

'Rascal,' she said softly.

However, this did nothing to ease Daniel's worries. Absently patting Vaishali as she stretched on the ground with her head in his lap, he went back to thinking of what he had not told anyone yet, even her.

Before he had quit the army, Daniel had been part of a division that undertook covert operations for the Research and Analysis Wing. The years of secret missions had sharpened his mind, which was why he could gauge certain things before anyone else. Ever since Marco had taken over the cruise liner, Daniel had carefully observed every move he and his men made. When the captives were led to the recreation hall, what had struck Daniel immediately was that the mercenaries seemed to be familiar with the layout of the vessel. Over the next seven days, Daniel mused over his initial hunch, slowly examining every angle.

He dismissed the idea that Marco and his men had carefully surveyed the cruise liner the night they had slipped aboard. They only had a three-hour window, which was simply too little time. Plus, there was always a chance of them being discovered by some guest.

Next, the mercenaries had no way of being sure that every guest aboard the cruise liner was asleep and in their rooms before they climbed aboard, even if they had been watching the cruise liner from afar using binoculars.

Their takeover of the ship's crew had also gone off too smoothly. The ship's crew would have been well-trained in measures to take in such contingencies, which would include sounding off some kind of an alarm or sending a distress signal. The hijackers had made sure none of that happened, and takeovers worked this effectively only when the perpetrators had two things on their side: the element of surprise and all the information necessary.

It was the second thing that bothered Daniel the most. The mercenaries seemed to have had too much information before they even set foot aboard the cruise liner. Which meant that there was a high chance they had inside help, a mole aboard the cruise liner. Which meant that apart from coming up with a plan to save everyone on board, Daniel also had to identify the mole. And he had no idea how much time he had left.

# 20

*Friday afternoon, Mumbai.*

Among the many qualities that Mirza and Vikrant were famous for was their seemingly endless patience. Where others fretted and fumed, the mentor-protégé duo calmly ploughed ahead, choosing to focus on the solution rather than the problem.

That patience came in handy at the NIA office in Mumbai that afternoon as Mirza and Vikrant sat in a conference room going through reams of paperwork. They were examining reports sent by SP Devendra Kumar of the Bhopal Central Jail about the movements and interactions of the IM Five, as they had now come to be known by the police, over the last six months. The SP had personally put together the report after interviewing all the guards who had come in contact with the five.

Three days after Mirza had apprised the Maharashtra DGP of the '93 Cache situation, Vikrant had been racking his brains over a cigarette on the terrace of the NIA building. He had been forbidden to go out of the building unless, in Mirza's words, 'You staying in the building would directly result in the loss of human life.' He remembered something else that Mirza had told him in their initial days of working together, 'There will always be one direction where you haven't looked hard enough. If everything else fails, find this direction and look again.'

In this case, the direction turned out to be backwards.

Vikrant suddenly remembered the reports on the movements and interactions of the IM Five that the officers at the Bhopal Central Jail had sent. At the time, the tip-off from his informant, Kamran Sheikh, about Asad's uncle, had put everything else on the backburner. He realized that the investigating team had never studied the reports, which had been hurriedly put together in the first place. As he flicked ash from his cigarette, he called Devendra Kumar and asked for the reports to be compiled again, in more detail this time. 'You can send them one by one, but keep them coming,' Vikrant told him.

And so it was that on the eighth day of Maharashtra going on high alert, Vikrant and Mirza sat across from each other at a long table in the conference room, each holding a report in his hand. Two laptops and a printer were set up in the room so that reports could be printed the moment Kumar emailed them from Bhopal.

Goyal and Jaiswal, meanwhile, were going through reports of all the Mahindra Boleros stolen in Bhopal over the last three months. The forensic technicians had pulled a partial licence plate from the burned-out remains of the SUV at Palghar, which showed that it was registered in Bhopal.

Mankame – whom Mirza had drafted into his team – was studying the background of Advocate Aslam Parkar, who had been representing the IM Five after their arrest.

'Assuming that the ISI got word to those five, setting the ball rolling, it must have been the lawyer who played postman. No one else would be in a better position, and their interactions with outsiders were restricted anyway,' Mirza had said after listening to Vikrant's idea of looking in a different direction.

The problem was that Parkar was known to be a clean lawyer, one of the few who truly believed in justice and ensuring a fair trial for everyone. In an age where defence lawyers had turned exploiting loopholes in the law into an art form, everybody who knew Parkar swore that his mission in life was only to ensure that the prosecution did not cut corners. He had chosen to represent the IM Five simply because he knew that terror accused were seen as terrorists by all and sundry even before being convicted, and he did not want that perception to decide their fate.

Mirza and Vikrant had both locked horns with Parkar in the past, and to think that someone like him could be connected with the ISI was next to impossible. However, both cops had seen stranger things and hence, Mankame was instructed to run an objective eye over Parkar's life.

However, none of the three junior cops were as patient as their seniors. Jaiswal's leg was bouncing up and down at a supersonic speed, which irritated Goyal. He would snap at Jaiswal roughly every half an hour and the latter would snap back. They would argue like kids till Mirza would silence them with a warning 'Lads…' or 'Boys!'

Mankame, after two hours of poring over Parkar's life, had stepped out for a smoke. 'I need some bloody nicotine in my system or else I'm going to scream,' he was heard muttering on his way out. Vikrant asked Mankame to get a pack for him as well and Mirza shot the former a look of extreme disapproval.

Only Vikrant and Mirza seemed to be their usual calm selves.

'Look at this,' Vikrant said, sliding a report forward. 'Three months ago, Parkar sent another lawyer to fill in for him during a routine hearing.'

'So?' Mirza asked, looking up from his own report.

'So, Parkar has always attended court in person in terror cases. He shuttles from his house in Pune wherever he needs to, once he's taken a personal interest in the case. I can recount at least … five instances, I think, in this trial alone, when he simply did not turn up and the hearing was adjourned. But he's never let anyone else appear.'

Mirza exhaled thoughtfully. 'I remember noticing this about him when he was defence for that case we had three years ago. He's got an ailing mother. He never talks about it because he hates people pitying him, but she sometimes has to be rushed to the hospital,' he said.

Vikrant nodded. 'The illegal arms case. He didn't turn up for some three or four hearings. The prosecutor even asked him to let a partner or employee fill in for him, to which he flatly refused.'

'And yet…' Mirza picked up the report Vikrant had just read. 'Rishabh Chawla. Ever heard this man's name before?' he asked, loud enough so that Goyal and Jaiswal could hear. They both shook their heads.

'Fuck,' Vikrant said. 'ISI bought Parkar?'

'Either bought or blackmailed. See if this Chawla fellow makes any more appearances in the story,' Mirza said, turning to the door just as Mankame walked in.

'You're going to Pune,' Mirza told Mankame.

'But give me my cigarettes first,' Vikrant added.

# 21

*Friday night, Lakshadweep.*

Years of covert operations in enemy territory had sharpened Daniel's instincts till he could sense trouble a mile away. As he lay on his back in the dark with his eyes open, his instincts told him that something was brewing.

It was the night of their ninth day in captivity. Earlier in the day, Marco and all his men had silently trooped into the room, a little after the captives had finished their breakfast and the kitchen crew had returned.

The hostages tensed up as Marco, casually holding his Uzi, strode to the centre of the room and ran a lazy eye over them.

'Everybody eat well?' he asked, smiling pleasantly. Nobody spoke.

'Good,' he went on. 'So in the next two minutes, I want everybody to form a straight line. After that, y'all walk up to the top deck with me without doin' anythin' stupid. If everybody behaves, this will be over before y'all know it.'

Daniel had to approve of his technique. He had allowed everyone to settle into a fixed routine for several days and then suddenly caught them off guard, just after they had finished a meal. This guy was good, he thought. Whatever he was planning, he was not going to meet with any resistance.

Marco's men were already taking positions. Two of them stationed themselves inside the room on either side of the doors, while the others trooped outside. Daniel guessed that they were taking positions along the corridor and staircase leading up to the top deck.

The captives silently shuffled into a straight line, nervously glancing at each other. Captain Sahani was at the lead. Daniel let Vaishali get into the middle of the line and then slowly manoeuvred himself backwards so that he was at the end. Vaishali realized he was gone and anxiously looked around for him till she saw him. He quickly nodded to her and she turned around again. Daniel glanced at Marco to see if he was watching, but he was talking to his second-in-command, whose name, Daniel had learned by keeping his ears open, was Omar.

Marco finished conferring with Omar and turned around.

'Y'all ready?' he asked.

A few of the hostages nodded.

'Follow me,' he said.

As Vaishali crossed the door, gently supporting an elderly woman in front of her, the gunman on the left leaned a little too close to her for comfort and inhaled deeply, loud enough for Vaishali to hear. Daniel could almost see her cringe as she walked on, head down.

A video camera on a tripod had been set up in the middle of the top deck, and the captives were marched up to it, after which they were made to sit down in three rows. One of their captors then started recording, panning the camera slowly from left to right and back again, till he had captured the entire crowd. Then he switched off the camera, removed its memory card and handed it to Marco, who turned to the captives.

'Good job, everybody,' he said nodding in approval. 'Let's all stay cooperative like this, huh? Easy for everyone. Now I got some work to take care of, so please get in a single line and walk back down. My man here,' Marco gestured to Omar, 'will be right behind y'all.'

As they were getting back in a line, Sahani caught Daniel's eye and they both nodded. *Proof of life.*

This time Daniel got into the middle of the line, a few heads away from Vaishali, who was behind Hakimi. The old man turned towards her and smiled briefly. Silently, they walked downstairs and back into the recreational area, passing Marco's men at regular intervals.

Daniel kept an eye on Vaishali and, as she passed through the doors, he saw the gunman who had leaned close to her earlier put out a hand and brush her hip as she passed. This time, she looked at him sharply and he responded with an insolent smile. With visible effort, Vaishali turned her gaze in front and stiffly walked to one corner of the room. Daniel sat beside her and held her till she stopped shaking.

Which was why, twelve hours later, Daniel lay awake as everyone around him, including Vaishali, slept, expecting trouble any second.

Trouble didn't disappoint. About half an hour later, one of the sliding doors opened wide enough for a person to step through, and Daniel saw the silhouette of a henchman slip inside. Noiselessly, he picked his way over the sleeping hostages till he was standing over Vaishali. Daniel, who was lying about a foot away, had closed his eyes just before the henchman got there, and now he opened one eye just wide enough to see the man kneel down and clamp a hand over her mouth.

Vaishali snapped awake and started to struggle. The mercenary pulled out a stiletto knife from his boot and held it in front of her face. She seemed to go rigid with fear and complied as he pulled her to her feet and started dragging her towards the door, holding the knife at her throat and his other hand over her mouth.

Slowly, Daniel brought himself up to a crouch and judged the distance between himself and the light switches. He was about to spring to them when someone else beat him to it.

People in the room were jolted awake when the lights were suddenly thrown on one by one. Daniel, whose eyes adjusted to the light faster, thanks to his army training, still blinked several times before he could believe what he was seeing. Standing near the light switches, hands curled into fists, was Abdul Jabbar Hakimi.

The henchman's lust melted away into panic at the sight of the waking captives and he dropped his knife to the ground, reached behind him, and brought up his Uzi. Most of the other captives were on their feet by now.

'Any of you fuckers move, you get killed,' he snarled.

Daniel slowly circled around the crowd, watching as Hakimi roughly pushed two people out of his way and walked straight up to the henchman, who was waving the Uzi from left to right, still holding on to Vaishali.

'You want to kill me, you khabees?' Hakimi growled, standing about a foot away from the man's gun, who brought it up to face level.

'You testing me, you old motherfucker?' the henchman said.

In a steady voice, Hakimi said, 'Have not you read the chapter on women in the Quran? Men are the protector of women!'

The henchman stared uncomprehendingly but kept his gun poised.

'I will protect her from you,' Hakimi declared.

'Man, get the fuck away!' the henchman said, backing towards the door.

'You want to kill me?' Hakimi repeated, stepping forward. 'Do it. Do it, because while there is a single breath left in my body, I will stand in your path. And I will not allow you to touch her.'

Daniel had managed to worm his way through the crowd to the very edge of the gunman's line of sight, and was now slowly moving forward, his eyes on the man's trigger finger. He was standing on the balls of his feet, ready to pounce at the slightest sign of pressure on the trigger, when the doors to the room slid open.

Everyone turned to look, including the gunman, and Daniel took advantage of the moment to move even closer to him.

Marco was standing at the door, and this time he wasn't smiling.

# 22

Aslam Parkar's ancestral home in Pune stood behind the Aaina Masjid in Ganesh Peth, one of the many 'peths' or localities in the city.

A first-timer is sure to be confused by the sheer number of peths. There are over seventeen of them in Pune, established over 200 years ago during the time of the Peshwas of the Maratha regime. The names have remained unchanged since then.

Lighting a cigarette, DCP Ashok Mankame looked up at Parkar's modest one-storey house from across the street. He laughed to himself as he remembered how, on his first visit to Pune, he had ended up at Budhwar Peth, the city's red-light area, instead of Mangalwar Peth where he was supposed to go.

This time Mankame had done the smart thing. Before he'd left for Pune, he requested Mirza to put in a word to the Pune police commissioner. By the time he reached, he had received a call from the zonal DCP, the divisional ACP and the senior inspector of the Faraskhana police station, in whose jurisdiction Parkar's house was located.

A constable had been waiting for Mankame's car as it entered Pune. He took over from the driver, expertly navigating through the streets and bringing the vehicle to a halt outside the police station within an hour. Mankame told SI Ravikant Phadke what he needed and fifteen minutes later, both cops were on their way to Parkar's house.

The house was locked when they got there, and three of Parkar's neighbours told the policemen that they had seen Parkar put his mother into an ambulance and leave in the middle of the night roughly a couple of weeks ago. Mankame quizzed them some more and in the end, all three of them agreed that it had been exactly fourteen days earlier. Like any good cop, a small alarm went off in Mankame's head.

'Has there been any word from him after that?' he inquired.

'No, sir,' one of the neighbours, a middle-aged man with a huge paunch, said.

'Is he usually out of touch like this when his mother is hospitalized?' Mankame asked.

'Come to think of it, no. He always calls one of us so that we can use the spare key and get the house dusted whenever he is gone for a long time. He likes to have it cleaned before his mother is moved back. Dust affects her.'

'And where is this spare key?' Mankame asked.

The man went back into his house and came out with the spare key a minute later. Mankame took it from him and was about to unlock Parkar's house when Phadke politely intervened. 'I'm sorry, sir, but I just need to be sure that there is a really strong reason to enter his house without his permission.'

Mankame turned around to look at the junior cop, who shifted uneasily.

'Just … you know… I'll have to answer to my DCP later … in case Parkar takes objection or something…' he said.

'Phadke, Parkar and his mother have been missing since the day that five of his clients, accused of terror, broke out of Bhopal Central Jail. Is that a strong enough reason for you?'

Phadke's face changed.

'Want me to call a forensic team or something?' he asked.

'Let's find out,' Mankame said and turned the key.

The spacious living room was flanked by a kitchen on one side and a bedroom on the other, while a staircase at the far end led to the first floor. A thin sheet of dust coated everything in the house. Mankame and Phadke split up, scanning the bedroom and kitchen respectively. Phadke completed a search of the kitchen, finding nothing of interest, and went to the bedroom, which Mankame was already scanning.

The Mumbai cop was holding a pack of cigarettes in his hand as Phadke entered.

'Want a light?' Phadke asked.

'These aren't mine,' Mankame answered, pulling out his cellphone and dialling Mirza.

'Yes, Mankame?' Mirza answered on the third ring.

'Does Parkar smoke?' Mankame asked.

There was silence on the other end, after which Mankame heard Mirza talking to Vikrant.

'No, he doesn't,' Mirza said. 'What's happening there?'

Mankame told him about Parkar's disappearance and listened intently before hanging up.

'Call that forensic team,' he told Phadke.

Now, as he waited for the forensic team to complete its search, his mind began racing. While they had been waiting for the forensic team to arrive, Mankame had asked Phadke to find out which hospital Parkar's mother was usually taken to and check if she had been admitted there over the last two weeks.

He was pretty certain that the answer would be in the negative, and so was Mirza. 'Better start checking on unidentified dead bodies found over the last fortnight,' Mirza told Mankame and he relayed the instruction to Phadke.

Meanwhile, various police officials started descending on the quiet locality. The divisional ACP arrived first, followed shortly by the zonal DCP and a team from the local Crime Branch unit, and then the DCP of the Crime Branch. Soon, Mankame observed a tacit struggle for control over the crime scene as the city police and the Crime Branch competed to grab vital clues so that they could solve the disappearance of the prominent lawyer and his mother first.

Mankame shook his head resignedly. As one of the two DCPs of the Mumbai Crime Branch, he had often done the same, pushing his officers to solve an important case before the local police station could. For the first time, he found himself disapproving of the practice.

Pulling out his phone, he again had a word with Mirza, who told him to stay put. Mankame waited for twenty minutes before Phadke came up to him.

'The CP just called, sir. You are officially in charge of this investigation and we are to assist you in any way you want us to,' he said.

Mankame rejoiced inwardly and glanced over Phadke's shoulder, watching the two DCPs leave the spot, followed by the ACP.

'How good is the Crime Branch unit head?' he asked Phadke.

Reluctantly, Phadke said, 'Quite good, sir. Experienced and has a good information network.'

'Apart from him and you, I want everyone else out of here. Ask some constables to stay back in case we need them. But no one else.'

Phadke nodded and walked back to the house just as the head of the forensic team walked up to him.

'Who's in charge?' he asked. Phadke inclined his head towards Mankame.

The forensics expert held up a small transparent plastic bag.

'Found this in the upper bedroom, under the bed,' he said.

Inside the bag was a spent pistol shell.

# 23

*Saturday afternoon, Lakshadweep.*

'What do you think they are going to do?' Hakimi asked.

'I don't know,' Daniel mused. 'Whatever they want, it's not money.'

'Take a guess?' Vaishali said.

They were sitting in a corner of the recreational area. It was late afternoon and most of the captives were asleep. There wasn't much else to do.

After the previous night's episode, Hakimi had become something of a hero among his fellow passengers. Marco, after taking a look at the spectacle in front of him, had wordlessly stared at his man till he had let Vaishali go. Marco then nodded to the door and the man quietly walked out. Marco, too, turned and followed him out.

Nobody could go back to sleep after that. Vaishali had run to Daniel, who hugged her tightly, while other women in the group milled around, comforting her. Leaving her in the care of the women, Daniel had walked over to Hakimi and held out his hand.

'Thank you,' he said.

Hakimi took his hand and gave it a firm shake.

'We got off on the wrong foot,' Daniel continued. 'Fresh start?'

Hakimi smiled and nodded.

'Fresh start,' he echoed. They both walked over to Vaishali.

Till the next morning both men sat side by side, while Vaishali lay with her head on Daniel's lap. They talked for hours, Hakimi telling Daniel about his experiences as a history teacher in a college in Mumbai before his retirement, Daniel recounting incidents from his time in the army.

'I still don't know how you managed to beat me to the light switches though,' Daniel said, curiously.

'I was right next to them. The gunman accidentally nudged me with his foot while going over to Vaishali. I saw everything that happened and couldn't just lie there and do nothing,' he explained.

Every once in a while, Vaishali, who was dozing fitfully, would wake up with a start and both men would calm her down.

'You are a good person, Mr Fernando,' Hakimi said after watching Daniel put Vaishali back to sleep for the third time.

'It's Daniel,' he said softly, smiling. 'And so are you. Not many people would have done what you did.'

'You looked like you were about to do something,' Hakimi said.

'You noticed?' Daniel asked. 'It's different with me. I have training, experience ... the rest of the people here, they've led different lives ... apart from you and me, do you think anyone else would have stepped forward?'

'You never know,' Hakimi said. 'All it takes is one brave soul.'

Daniel nodded.

'My first ever mission was in Kargil, during the war. I was scared as hell, and just following orders. Within the first hour, we had lost all three of our senior officers. It was just us – a bunch of fresh recruits who were seeing combat for the first time.'

'What happened?'

'I took charge. I had no idea if I was doing the right thing. I had no idea what I was doing, actually. But someone had to. And I couldn't just wait and hope that someone else would.'

'And?'

'We made it.' Daniel grinned. 'Somehow, we finished our mission and made it back alive.'

Hakimi grinned back at him.

'As I said, all it takes is one brave soul.'

The next morning, another one of their captors entered the room and led the kitchen crew up to the cafeteria as usual. An hour later, Sahani too was led to the engine room.

When he came back, he told Daniel that there was no sign of Vaishali's molester.

'I even tried asking Marco when he came to the engine room. He just smiled and told me to mind my own business,' Sahani reported.

Daniel had been keeping an eye on the view through the portholes and could make out that the cruise liner had been making all its scheduled halts at various islands in

Lakshadweep and waiting for enough time to pass before moving on. Sahani went back up to the engine room after lunch and Vaishali slid down on the floor with Daniel on one side and Hakimi on the other.

'Whatever they are planning, they will have to do it fast. According to the cruise schedule, we're supposed to turn back for Mumbai today. If we don't, someone will smell a rat,' Daniel reasoned just as the door slid open and Sahani walked in.

All three looked towards him but only Daniel sensed that something was wrong. He waited for the door to be shut before walking over to Sahani. Vaishali and Hakimi followed him.

'Something happen?' he asked.

'The radio,' Sahani replied. 'They destroyed the radio.'

'Destroyed it?' Vaishali asked, surprised.

Sahani nodded.

'Put a bullet into it. We've been told to drop anchor till further instructions.'

Daniel took a deep breath.

'It's happening,' he said. 'Whatever they're planning, it has begun.'

# 24

*Saturday morning–Sunday morning, Bhopal.*

The same morning that Mankame left for Pune, Mirza had sent DSPs Goyal and Jaiswal to Bhopal to dig up more dirt on Rishabh Chawla, the lawyer who had filled in for Parkar thrice.

The cops started with the guards who had escorted the IM Five to prison and back, but they were not of much help. They remembered seeing another lawyer in Parkar's place, but could not provide much of a description. With the help of the Bhopal police, Goyal got in touch with some lawyers who regularly had cases in the same courtroom as the IM Five, and two of them remembered interacting with Chawla.

'We found it strange because Parkar has never sent someone else in his place. Chawla didn't say much and left immediately after the hearing. He was speaking softly with his clients for quite some time, though,' one of them said.

Jaiswal, meanwhile, contacted the public prosecutor in the case, a seasoned lawyer named Prakash Yadav.

'Oh yes, Rishabh Chawla. Quiet chap. Told me that Parkar's mother was worse than usual. Actually hinted at the fact that she might not be with us for very long. How is she, any idea?' Yadav asked.

Jaiswal said that he didn't and steered the subject back to Chawla.

'Well, he said he was from Pune, which is how he knows Parkar. Told me he was doing Parkar a favour.'

'You wouldn't have a phone number for him, would you?' Jaiswal asked.

'Actually, I do. I asked for it in case I needed to contact him for anything,' Yadav replied.

Jaiswal obtained the call data records of the number that Chawla had given Yadav for the days that Chawla was in Bhopal and studied its cellular locations, which showed that Chawla had been in the Arera Hills area for the first half of the day of the hearing and then moved towards Gandhi Nagar, where the central jail was located.

Jaiswal expanded his search and asked for call detail records of the number for the previous two months, starting from three days before Chawla first appeared in court on Parkar's behalf.

Goyal, meanwhile, contacted the Maharashtra Bar Council. By evening, an official from the council called him back to tell him that they had no records of any lawyer named Rishabh Chawla.

Both the officers stayed up till late in the night, analysing the cellular movements of the number that Chawla had given Parkar, their excitement rising as the night passed. They slept at dawn and woke up four hours later to resume their work.

After another hour, their analysis was complete and Goyal called up Mirza.

'Whoever this man was, he's definitely not a simple lawyer, sir,' he said.

'Tell me more, lad,' Mirza said.

'Well, the first time he came to Bhopal, he initially went to the Sessions Court, where he posed as a replacement for Parkar. He then went towards the central jail and spent a good three hours in the area. I'm guessing he was doing a recce.'

'Go on.'

'Pretty much repeated the routine the next two times. He stayed for two days on his second visit and left immediately after the court appearance on his third visit, which was five days before the jailbreak.'

'Do we know where he was staying during these visits?'

'Not yet, sir. Assuming he was ISI, maybe he stayed with a sleeper agent?'

'Maybe. But if I were him, I'd want to maintain my cover completely. We know more about sleeper agents than our neighbours think, and most, if not all of them, are under surveillance. A lawyer from Pune staying with a sleeper agent would ring alarm bells.'

'Really, sir? We know who these bastards are?' Goyal asked.

'It is an age-old game that intelligence agencies across the world play with each other,' Mirza explained. 'Each country lets the other think that it is in the dark while actually keeping a careful eye on their agents, moving in only when one of them is about to cause some real damage.'

'Want me to check hotels and lodges near his location? He was mostly in Gandhi Nagar but would return to Arera Hills at night. Maybe he was staying at a hotel there.'

'Go for it,' Mirza said.

Goyal, with the help of the local police, drew up a list of hotels in Arera Hills, while Jaiswal went to visit Prakash Yadav along with a sketch artist. Within an hour, the sketch artist, whom the NIA had used in the past, skilfully drew out a portrait of Chawla from Yadav's description.

'It's not much, but it'll have to do,' the artist said, handing over the sketch to Jaiswal.

The two NIA officers then commandeered a team of twenty-five constables from the Bhopal police, deputed thanks to a call by Mirza to the Bhopal police commissioner, and sent one constable to each hotel in Arera Hills, armed with a copy of the sketch and the dates on which Chawla was in Bhopal.

Then they waited, Jaiswal bouncing his leg up and down and Goyal snapping at him every few minutes, till one of the constables called back. Jaiswal made a mad lunge for his cellphone.

'We found him, sir,' the constable said. 'He stayed at this hotel during his first two visits. I think you said he didn't stay the night the third time so...'

'What have you found?' Jaiswal cut in.

'An address in Pune, a PAN card photocopy and a photograph that the desk manager took as part of their procedure...'

Jaiswal punched the air and whooped loudly.

# 25

*Sunday afternoon, Mumbai.*

Mirza sat at his desk at the NIA office in Mumbai with his laptop in front of him, staring at the picture of Rishabh Chawla that Goyal had emailed him. He kept staring for another five minutes before minimizing the image and opening his browser.

Mirza had entered the world of intelligence when the digital age was in its early days. He had written out official reports on typewriters and used pagers on the field, and had reluctantly turned to using computers when they became common. Realizing the importance of the digital medium, he had asked one of the in-house software experts at IB to create a secret encrypted storage space on his computer, which he could access any time he wanted.

The expert had had a better idea. He had hacked a semi-popular blog by a woman who wrote about her experiences as a single mother, and made a secret backdoor that only Mirza and he could access, using a password. Mirza could log into the blog using a different name and password, and the woman, blissfully unaware, could continue to blog about her toddler's antics. With the kind of traffic she was getting, the chances of her shutting down the blog were next to nil. Mirza just had to visit the blog regularly in case she posted an update about moving it to a different platform.

'That way, you don't need to worry about your computer being hacked and don't need to carry the info with you all the time on an external storage device,' the expert had told him.

'What's an external storage device?' Mirza had asked.

Now, as Mirza logged in to the blog, he was mildly excited.

After 26/11, Mirza, who was in the IB at the time, had set up a team to go through every bit of news media coverage, be it TV, print or online. The team had gone through lakhs of pictures and videos taken around the targets sites during the attacks and one of the members, Norman D'Souza, noticed a pattern. The same man was partially visible in a lot of the visuals of the vicinity of the target sites.

Mirza, after being notified, had asked Norman to track this man further and in twenty-four hours, the team had tracked his movements from the Leopold Cafe to the Taj Mahal Hotel, the Oberoi-Trident, Chhatrapati Shivaji Terminus and Chabad House.

'He's making an effort to hide, sir,' Norman told Mirza. 'He either turns away from news cameras whenever they pan his way or raises one hand to his face or something. The best we have is this.'

Mirza picked up the printout that Norman handed him. It showed the man looking away from a television news camera.

He must have not known about the still photographer right behind him and ended up facing him, Mirza thought.

The face was partially turned towards the still camera but the lighting was bad, as it was shot at night. Mirza spoke to a few of his trusted contacts in the Mumbai police and told them what he needed. It took seven days but one of his cops ultimately found a CCTV camera in Colaba that had captured the man walking past while on his way to Leopold. Mirza confirmed the direction he had come from. It was Badhwar Park, from where the ten terrorists had entered the city.

Using the still that Norman had given him and the footage of the camera, Mirza got his experts to put together a composite image. He then shared it with his contacts in the intelligence and surveillance community the world over and asked for any information on the mystery man. Within an hour, he started getting responses from foreign agencies who had similar pictures of him. Facial recognition technology identified him as the same man. Whether at a blast site in Tel Aviv or the scene of a gun battle in Beirut, he was always among the onlookers who were gathered at the site of any terrorist attack.

Mirza probed further but found little information. Deep cover agents in Asia and the Middle East had heard of a man who was so committed to the cause of the global Caliphate that he would leave no stone unturned while planning his missions. He was said to be the uncredited brain behind scores of terror strikes, a master of disguise, utterly ruthless and thoroughly dangerous. Other reports said that he had an elaborate cover set up, thanks to which he led a perfectly normal life even while conducting the orchestra of terror across the continent. His ability to manage two personalities at the same time was said to be chilling. In Islamic terminology and Quranic verses, such men are referred to as Munafiq – hypocrites who masquerade as believers but are actually hidden enemies.

Praying hard, Mirza logged in to his storage space through the backdoor and opened the file he was looking for. He spent a long time studying the pictures put together by various intelligence agencies.

He tore his eyes away from the screen just as Vikrant came bursting through the door. Walking swiftly up to Mirza's desk, Vikrant laid down several pages next to each other for his mentor to look at.

Vikrant had spoken to Goyal and Jaiswal, who were now on their way back to Mumbai and after listening to a detailed report of their activities, had asked Jaiswal to email him all CDRs of Rishabh Chawla's number. He had then gone through the entire data and identified five numbers that Chawla had dialled the most and sought their cellular locations during the period that they were in touch with Chawla. He had received the reports ten minutes ago.

'Chawla was in constant touch with these five people,' Vikrant told Mirza. 'And they spent all the time they were in contact in Pune. They never moved out of Ganesh Peth, where Parkar lived. How much do you want to bet that these five men were holding Parkar and his mother hostage while Chawla was setting up the jailbreak in Bhopal?'

Vikrant glanced up from the CDR reports and saw the look on Mirza's face.

'Okay,' he asked. 'What?'

Wordlessly, Mirza turned his laptop around.

'O… okay…' Vikrant said, perplexed, looking at the photos in Mirza's secret storage. 'And…?'

'Switch tabs,' Mirza told him.

Vikrant hit Alt+ Tab and found himself staring at the picture of Rishabh Chawla sent by the hotel manager in Bhopal. He switched tabs at least ten times before he could believe that he was looking at the same man.

'Fuck,' he said, sinking into a chair. 'Munafiq?'

At that instant the landline started ringing.

# 26

*Sunday afternoon, Mumbai.*

'You really don't know why the CM wants to see you?' Mankame asked.

'He didn't say,' Mirza growled.

Mankame had returned from Pune an hour ago and was entering the NIA office when he spotted Mirza and Vikrant walking out. Mirza signalled him to come with them, and Mankame followed.

They all got into an NIA car. 'To the Mantralaya, and step on it,' Mirza barked at Mankame.

While he and Vikrant were sitting stunned at their discovery, Mirza had received a call from the chief minister of Maharashtra, Yashwant Pradhan. He had simply asked Mirza to meet him immediately and to bring Vikrant with him.

Mirza had people in various agencies that he could have called and found out why the CM wanted to see him, but his mind was still racing with the implications of one of the most dangerous terrorists in Asia having come to India two months ago, and possibly still hiding somewhere in the country. So he just sat looking out of the window, thinking hard, while Vikrant brought Mankame up to speed.

'What was that word again?' Mankame asked.

'Munafiq,' Vikrant replied as they entered the Mantralaya compound. 'It's the Urdu word for two-faced. Someone who assumes an identity but is actually somebody else.'

Mankame had more questions, but they had reached the parking lot by then. Mirza asked Mankame to wait in the car and jumped out even before the car came to a stop. Vikrant hurried after him.

The CM's personal secretary was waiting outside the building for them. Quickly, they got into the lift and made their way up to his office. Chief Minister Yashwant Pradhan was sitting at his desk, while State Home Minister Sudarshan Raskar stood at the window.

'*Tashreef rakhiye, Mirza sahab*,' Pradhan said, trying to flaunt his Urdu, as both Mirza and Vikrant saluted the two politicians. Raskar turned around but didn't say anything. From past experience, Vikrant knew that this was a bad sign.

'So,' Pradhan began as he dismissed his secretary. 'What I'm telling you doesn't leave the room. This is very important, so feel free to ask questions wherever you need to. Okay?'

Both cops nodded. Pradhan looked at Raskar, who cleared his throat and started talking.

'Yesterday afternoon, a cruise liner from Mumbai to Lakshadweep suddenly went incommunicado. When their control room failed to get them on the radio repeatedly, they alerted the Coast Guard, who sent a chopper to its last-known location.

'The Coast Guard found the liner anchored off Lakshadweep under the control of armed men. Our first impression was that they're Somali pirates, but the Coast Guard disagree, saying they look well-built, combat-trained and what not. Anyway, one of the pirates, for want of a better word, used a strong flashlight to signal to the chopper in Morse code, asking for one man to be sent to the liner's deck. After some discussion, the Coast Guard agreed and one of their personnel was dropped onto the deck last evening using a rope. The pirate told him that everyone was alive and well and gave him this,' Raskar finished, sliding a flash drive on the table over to Mirza.

Pradhan gestured to a laptop on his desk, and Mirza plugged in the flash drive to see two video files inside.

The first video was shot using a Handycam and had men, women and some children sitting in an uneven formation on the top deck of the cruise liner. The camera panned slowly across them from left to right and back before it was turned off.

The second video had a dark-skinned, stockily built Somali standing on the top deck with the sea behind him. It was impossible to judge where the liner was when it was taken. The man, after waiting for five seconds, started speaking.

'My name is Marco. Y'all probably have files on me somewhere, so please read 'em and know that I mean business. I got thirty people from your country in this li'l boat and I have enough men with guns and plenty of bullets to use on each one of your citizens for target practice till they all die. So when I ask for somethin', you give it.'

Marco held up a large piece of cardboard with a number written on it.

'Call me on this satellite phone at exactly 9 p.m., your time,' he said and the screen went blank.

For half a minute, nobody spoke. Then Mirza looked at Pradhan.

'Did we look up this Marco's file?' Mirza asked.

'We did. And if you're wondering why you didn't hear about it,' Pradhan said, 'it's because PMO wanted a tight lid on it. Nobody was kept in the loop. And I mean nobody. Only one person was asked to look up Marco's file and report directly to the PMO.'

'And why is the PMO taking such an interest in a hijacked cruise liner?' Vikrant spoke up.

Pradhan and Raskar exchanged glances.

'We don't know,' Pradhan admitted. 'We've just been told to follow orders without asking questions.'

'Anyway, this Marco is a really evil character. He's a mercenary from Somalia credited with hundreds of kills all over the world. He's something of a favourite with fringe terrorist organizations and apparently he's been used by some intelligence agencies for their operations as well,' Raskar added.

'I'm assuming we called him at 9?' Mirza asked.

'We did,' Raskar said.

'And?' Mirza asked impatiently.

Pradhan looked sheepish.

'The PM said he'll tell you and Vikrant personally after I brief you,' he said. 'There's a dedicated hotline in my antechamber and he is waiting for your call.'

Both the cops, as they stood up to go to Pradhan's antechamber, found themselves trying to think of a stronger word for bewildered to describe their state of mind.

Mirza led the way inside and Vikrant followed, after which they walked over to a side table bearing a phone.

'Please tell me you have some idea of what's going on,' Vikrant asked his mentor.

Mirza only shook his head before picking up the phone. He looked at the list of hotline numbers on the table and dialled the PM. The call was answered on the first ring.

'This is Mirza, sir,' he said.

For the next two minutes, Vikrant watched as Mirza listened intently, saying nothing more than 'yes, sir', 'right, sir' and 'understood, sir', after which he hung up and turned around.

'Well?' Vikrant asked.

'Marco wants the IM Five to be taken to the cruise liner safely. And he wants you to do it.'

For a while, Vikrant and Mirza just stood staring at each other.

Finally, Vikrant spoke.

'But ... but we don't know where they are!'

'Marco does,' Mirza told him.

# 27

*Sunday evening, Mumbai.*

As evening fell in Behrambaug, Jogeshwari, a group of men and women gathered at the buzzing tea stall in the middle of the locality. Simply called Rahim Chacha's Hyderabadi Chaiyy, it was the favourite hangout for the adults in the area, while the teenagers preferred other spots, away from the disapproving 'oldies'.

The centre of attention at the stall that evening was a pretty woman in her late thirties, who was regaling the locals with tales of her travels. Sonam Dhillon, an executive with a private research agency, had clearly seen the world.

For the last five days, Sonam and her team of five, all of them men, had been roaming through the entire slum, interacting with the locals and taking photographs for a survey they were conducting, based on which the state government was thinking of allocating funds for better facilities, such as improved roads, additional public toilets and regular water supply.

It took Sonam only a couple of days to win over the elders of the locality with her frank smile and charming manners. Once their blessings were obtained, the doors of Behrambaug opened up to the team. They would work from morning to night, and often take breaks at Rahim Chacha's tea stall. After their third day, Rahim Chacha even stopped charging them.

What no one in Behrambaug knew or suspected was that Sonam and her team were working on orders from the chief of the Intelligence Bureau. The same day that Shawaz Ali Mirza had had Shagufta Bi, the mother of Mustafa and Ibrahim Kadir from the IM Five, picked up and leaked the rumour of her being driven away from the area, he had called up the local IB chief and told him what he needed.

It was a sheer stroke of luck for Sonam and her team, who were trained IB officers, that Rahim Chacha's tea shack offered a direct view of the Kadir residence. Over the next few days, the supposed surveyors made sure that at least one of them was somewhere near the house when they were not taking breaks at the tea stall.

That evening, Sonam was telling the people about her experiences in Ballimaran while she had worked on 'a government-sanctioned report about heritage structures'. It was a necessary lie, as she could hardly tell the residents of Behrambaug that she had been tailing an ISI agent who was posing as a tourist in Old Delhi.

The rest of her team was keeping an eye on the Kadir residence. Sonam was just finishing an anecdote when one of her men, Rohan Awasthi, noticed an autorickshaw pull up outside the house. Gulping down the rest of his tea, he stood up, pulling out a pack of cigarettes from his shirt pocket.

'*Kahaan chale, Awasthi*?' Sonam asked. Awasthi held up his pack of cigarettes and Sonam made a disapproving noise.

Sticking a cigarette in his mouth, he wandered close to the Kadir house while fishing around in his pocket for a lighter. The autorickshaw driver was talking to a neighbour.

'No, I was just concerned,' the driver was saying. 'I called her a couple of times but could not reach her phone.'

'*Pata nahi, beta*,' the neighbour, an elderly woman, said. 'Some people had come at night. They took her away and we haven't seen her since.'

'Policemen?' the driver asked. Awasthi immediately pulled out his cellphone and sent a group message to his team. There was no reason for the driver to ask that unless he suspected that Shagufta's 'ouster' from the locality was orchestrated by the authorities. And there was no reason for him to be suspicious unless he was trained to think that way.

The neighbour repeated that she did not know, and that it had all happened very fast. The driver turned on his heel and got back into his autorickshaw. By the time he pulled out of the narrow lanes of the slum, one of Awasthi's colleagues was waiting at the junction leading to the main road on his motorbike. He smoothly pulled into the traffic behind the autorickshaw as it turned towards Dahisar.

Awasthi, meanwhile, went back to Sonam, interrupting her third tale of the evening, and told her that they were all needed 'at the office'. Sonam bid a cheery goodbye to the locals, who, though they did not know it then, would never see her again.

Sonam, Awasthi and their three colleagues walked to their vehicles, Sonam to a car while the others to two-wheelers. As soon as she got in, Sonam speed dialled Mirza on her cellphone.

'Stay on him,' Mirza said. 'Do not engage him, but don't you dare lose him.'

# 28

*Sunday evening, Mumbai.*

Mirza got off the phone with Sonam and walked back into the conference room.

After the meeting with Pradhan, Mankame had driven Mirza and Vikrant back to the office. On the way Vikrant told Mankame what transpired at the CM's office, while Mirza made phone call after phone call, rousing every source he had and asking them to give him whatever they knew about Marco and the cruise liner he had hijacked.

They got back to the office to find Jaiswal and Goyal waiting for them. Mirza asked the entire NIA Mumbai staff to leave immediately. 'No one apart from my team stays. If I need any of you, I'll call you,' he told them.

Once they were alone in the office, Mankame updated Jaiswal and Goyal about all the new developments, while the two DSPs listened with increasingly widening eyes and gaping mouths. Vikrant once again took pleasure in explaining the concept and import of the term 'Munafiq', duly impressing both officers.

After a brief discussion with his team, Mirza called the private number that the PM had given him. It took some convincing but the PM ultimately agreed to Mirza's proposition. Mirza's next call was to Maharashtra DGP Paramjeet Kalra. The top cop waited for an entire minute before reacting.

'Are you serious?' Kalra sputtered.

'I am, sir. If the IM Five are ready to leave, it means they are done with whatever they were planning with the '93 Cache. The city might erupt with bomb blasts the minute they leave. We really cannot take any chances. Please, please sound a red alert.'

There was silence at the other end.

'Find a way, Mirza,' Kalra said. 'Find a way to end this bloody thing.'

'I will, sir,' Mirza had promised.

Now, as Mirza came back to the conference room after his conversation with Sonam, he found his entire team in heated debate.

'What do you mean you're going alone?' Mankame snapped.

'I mean, I'm going alone,' Vikrant said calmly. 'They're in the middle of the sea. They'll see any approach miles away. I have to do what they say.'

'Why are you so eager to get killed?' Mankame said furiously.

'Let's not get morbid, Mankame,' Vikrant said.

Mankame stood up and stormed out. Goyal and Jaiswal, after a minute's hesitation, went after him.

Mirza stared intently at his protégé before going over and sitting on a chair near him.

'We'll find a way, lad,' he said.

Vikrant smiled.

'We always do, don't we, sir?'

For a few minutes, neither man spoke, each silently reflecting on the eight years they had worked together.

'We've come a long way, haven't we?' Vikrant said.

'Boy, if you start a goodbye speech, I swear I'll kill you myself,' Mirza threatened.

Vikrant chuckled and stood up.

'Let's go get the boys back,' he said.

Silently, they made their way up to the terrace.

'How do you know they'll be there?' Mirza asked.

'Well, Mankame needs a smoke and you won't let us smoke inside the office,' Vikrant replied.

True enough, they found Mankame smoking in one corner of the terrace, with Goyal and Jaiswal talking to him. They all turned as Mirza and Vikrant approached. Mankame took one look at Vikrant and turned his head away.

'Calmed down yet?' Vikrant asked, pulling out his own pack. Mankame said nothing.

'Look, I understand how you feel...'

'No, you don't,' Mankame interrupted. 'You saved my bloody life in Palghar back then. I'm not going to sit by and watch while you just saunter towards certain death.'

'Then don't,' Mirza said and everyone turned to him.

'Marco told the PM's guys that we are to call him at 8 tomorrow morning. That gives us...' Mirza paused to look at his watch, 'nine hours. Let's get back down and make sense of this bloody mess so that we can find a way to keep this ruffian alive.'

Vikrant took a last drag at his cigarette before throwing it to the ground.

They decided to take the stairs to the office and on their way down, Mirza now told them about the development from Behrambaug.

'We're just watching this auto driver for now?' Goyal asked.

'For now, yes. I'm getting constant updates. We need to see whom he makes contact with before we move in.'

They reached the office and filed into the conference room.

'All right,' Mirza said. 'Some days ago, when we were on the hunt for our five villains, I received an email from a friend about a commercial freighter that had passed through Somali waters and made an unscheduled stop. We take an interest in all things Somalia because of the whole piracy issue, so we keep getting these updates. Anyway, this freighter was picked up on satellites belonging to certain agencies. It had stopped for five minutes just off the coast of Somalia and then resumed its course.'

Mirza stood up and passed printouts around the table.

'After speaking to the PM, I asked for an update and got these. They are satellite images tracking the freighter from Somalia to Indian waters. The freighter stopped a hundred nautical miles away from the cruise liner's position eleven nights ago. Easy enough for someone to get to the cruise liner using a dinghy or something,' he said.

'These are CIA satellites, aren't they?' Vikrant asked and Mirza nodded.

'The buggers watch everyone,' Jaiswal remarked.

'So,' Mirza continued. 'CIA tracked the freighter as it went on its course toward Indonesia and used its ground agents to find it at the Indonesian port, based on the date of its docking. The same agents found out the details of the freighter, and guess where it is from.'

'Pakistan?' Mankame asked. Mirza smiled.

'It started from the Gwadar Port in Pakistan three days before it made that stop in Somali waters.'

'ISI,' Goyal exclaimed.

'Munafiq,' Vikrant said.

Mirza nodded at both in acknowledgment before continuing.

'So, CIA's been watching the freighter and it left Indonesia an hour after Marco first made contact. It is now steadily moving towards Lakshadweep, where the cruise liner is now docked.'

'Munafiq,' Vikrant said again.

'Yes,' Mirza said. 'That's what I thought.'

'Umm, what?' a bewildered Mankame said while Goyal and Jaiswal looked from mentor to protégé.

'He's got to be on that freighter,' Vikrant said.

# 29

*Monday morning, Mumbai.*

In hindsight, Vikrant had to admit that it was perfect.

The team had worked through the night before Mirza insisted that they catch some sleep at 3 in the morning.

'Whatever has happened so far is going to pale in comparison, once the curtain goes up tomorrow and whatever they have planned starts happening. We'll need the rest,' Mirza told them.

They all woke up at 7.30 a.m. and waited anxiously for the clock to strike 8. On the dot, Vikrant dialled the number Marco had shown in his video, with the speakerphone on.

'This is Marco,' the deep voice on the other end said.

'This is SP Vikrant Singh, NIA.'

'Suspended, from what I hear,' Marco said with a snigger.

'You'd asked me to call,' said Vikrant, unfazed.

'That's right. Now, listen carefully. I want you to bring the five men who escaped from jail earlier to the cruise liner. You'll come straight here from Mumbai by chopper and not make any stops along the way. No bugs, no hidden weapons, no tricks. I don't need to tell ya what I will do if you annoy me.'

'We don't have the power to agree to that,' Mirza interjected.

'Who's this?' Marco asked.

'My name is Shahwaz Ali Mirza…'

'Oh, right. You don't ever leave your boy on his own, do you? Next time you talk out of turn, I'm gonna shoot someone here in the kneecap. Clear?'

'Yes,' Mirza muttered.

'I don't know where those five men are,' Vikrant said.

'Oh, don't worry, buddy. They're waitin' for you at Taj Land's End Hotel in Bandra,' Marco said and the line went dead.

The entire team made a mad dash for the door and almost fell over each other as they crowded into the lift and ran to an SUV in the parking lot. Mankame sent the vehicle shooting down Cumballa Hill towards Bandra while Mirza briefed the prime minister.

'We have to go all out, sir,' Mirza said. 'We can't keep this quiet any more.'

The PM agreed and Mirza briefed Mumbai Police Commissioner Virendra Sinha and DGP Kalra, while Jaiswal briefed NIA chief T. Rangaswamy and Goyal spoke to IB and RAW. By the time the SUV crossed Dadar, the PM was speaking to the head of the National Security Guard base set up in Mumbai after the 26/11 attacks.

Vikrant, in the meantime, sat in his seat silently, marvelling at the genius behind the plan. The police had spent days looking in all the usual places – slum pockets, cheap lodges, even abandoned buildings where the IM Five could have been lying low. Instead, the five bastards were staying at a five-star hotel in one of the plushest areas of the city, the last place anyone would think of looking for them. *This had to be Munafiq's idea,* Vikrant thought. *Only he would have the audacity to pull off something like this.*

Five vehicles of the NSG came roaring up to the hotel almost at the same time that Mirza and his team got there. Mirza had his ID in his hands as he walked towards one of the NSG commandos, who were quickly setting up a perimeter around the hotel.

'Who's in charge?' Mirza asked.

'Guess?' said a voice behind him and Mirza turned to see a slim, petite woman in full commando regalia grinning at him.

'Bloody hell!' said Mirza happily as he recognized the face under the commando cap. 'Major Shaina Verma … it IS Major now, isn't it?'

'There's nothing you don't know, is there, sir?' Shaina said, smiling.

Mirza looked towards his SUV and saw Vikrant standing near the vehicle, his face looking like it was made of stone.

'Bloody hell,' he repeated, softly this time. Shaina turned around and stiffened as she saw Vikrant.

'What is he doing here?' she hissed.

'What did your seniors tell you?'

'Just that we were needed here, and that you would tell us the rest of it,' she said, under her breath.

'Yeah, well, he is the rest of it,' Mirza said, after which he brought her up to speed.

Shaina listened with growing disbelief before saying, 'And this is not your idea of some mock drill?'

'How I wish it were, girl.' Mirza sighed.

Shaina took a deep breath.

'Right,' she said. 'Let's get this over with.'

She marched up to Vikrant, Mirza behind her.

'Mr Singh,' she said stiffly.

'Major,' he replied.

'You ready?'

He nodded. At that moment Shaina's earpiece crackled and she turned to the entrance of the hotel. Mirza and Vikrant followed her lead and saw a man in a formal suit standing with his arms raised.

'Everybody stay back,' Shaina said into her walkie-talkie. She raised her MP5 sub-machine gun and slowly advanced towards the man, Mirza and Vikrant following her.

'You stay here,' she told them.

'Sorry, Major,' Vikrant said. 'But I have a feeling that that man is standing there for me. And I'm not about to waste time.'

Vikrant started walking towards the man.

'For fuck's sake,' Shaina breathed, throwing a look of exasperation towards Mirza, who just shrugged.

She beckoned Mirza to follow him and jogged up to Vikrant, falling into step ahead of him, her weapon raised.

'Stay behind me,' she hissed at Vikrant and Mirza.

The man stood sweating till the trio reached him.

'Who are you?' Shaina demanded.

'Deepak Mukherjee. I'm the manager here,' the man replied, trembling.

'What do you want?' Shaina continued.

'There are five men sitting in the lobby. One of them came up to me some ten minutes ago and told me that the hotel was going to be surrounded by the police and military. He told me to ask for Vikrant Singh when that happened.'

Shaina stepped sideways, not taking her gun off Mukherjee, and Vikrant came forward.

'I'm Vikrant,' he said.

'He said to tell you that you are to come inside alone and unarmed.'

'He give a name?' Mirza asked.

'Yes ... he said his name is Usman Qureshi.'

# 30

Those who knew Vikrant knew that he hardly ever smiled. Some put this down to the scars left behind by 26/11. While this was true, there was also another reason behind it.

Only Mirza knew why, three years after 26/11, Vikrant had almost stopped smiling altogether.

By then Vikrant, working closely under Mirza's tutelage in the IB, had become well versed in spy craft and had been hounding his mentor for his first solo mission. After a lot of reluctance, Mirza had agreed, but on one condition.

'I don't need a babysitter,' Vikrant had complained.

'You're an investigator, lad,' Mirza had explained. 'Not a warrior. You'll meet Captain Verma from the NSG, who's on deputation with us for a while, near the Wagah border tomorrow, and proceed on your mission.'

'Captain Verma' had turned out to be a petite young woman with raven-black hair and almond-shaped brown eyes. The

139

fact that the mission was a covert one and Shaina was not in uniform brought out her beauty all the more.

Vikrant and Shaina spent six days together, tracking an ISI agent who had come across the border posing as a truck driver bringing in cement from Pakistan. Instead of taking the truck to the wholesale market, however, the man had just parked it at a desolate spot on the highway, got into a car waiting next to it and started driving towards Amritsar.

'Now?' Shaina asked, noticing that there were almost no cars on the stretch of the highway at the time.

'I don't see why not,' Vikrant said from the driver's seat of their Jeep.

Without a moment's hesitation, Shaina drew a silenced 9mm while Vikrant stepped on the accelerator. They were almost abreast of the target's car when Shaina pulled the trigger twice. Both bullets hit the rear right wheel and the car flew into the air.

Braking hard, Vikrant pulled to the side of the road and they both waited for the car to hit the ground upside down before running towards it.

Shaina stood guard while Vikrant went down on all fours and pulled the target out of the mangled remains of the car. He was trying to say something, but Vikrant wasn't interested. He calmly reached around the man and pulled his backpack out of the car. Then he fished around in his pockets till he found his cellphone and pocketed it. Moving quickly, he whipped out a small knife and pried both the bullets out of the rear tyre.

'What about the shell casings?' Shaina asked.

Vikrant made a dismissive gesture.

'Not enough time to look for them,' he said as they ran back to their Jeep. 'Plus it's getting dark and I don't think anyone's going to be looking for shell casings at an "accident" site.'

'Smart,' Shaina said, punching Vikrant lightly on the shoulder as she slid in next to him. They sped away and went straight to a hotel in Ludhiana, where a suite had already been booked for them.

An hour later, a man met them in the hotel lobby and took the backpack as well as the target's cellphone.

'Lie low,' he told them. 'There are people looking for you.'

They ended up spending a week at the hotel, and that week changed Vikrant's life. They were sharing the suite, posing as a couple, and would spend their days in one of the many restaurants or bars in the hotel, or in the pool area, racking up a hefty bill for the Indian government. By their third day together, Vikrant was madly in love with Shaina, who shared his burning sense of patriotism and had seen as much evil as he had.

They would talk for hours together about their lives, past and present, in the day, and make tender love at night, lying in each other's arms till they fell asleep.

Over the next two months, they saw each other as often as they could and with each passing day, Vikrant was increasingly convinced that he had finally met someone he was ready to get serious with.

That was till the day Shaina told him that her ex-boyfriend of four years, whom she had broken up with just before she met Vikrant, had asked for one last chance to make things work, and she had agreed. Vikrant was too shocked to even respond.

He had simply stood up and walked away, leaving her sitting alone in the restaurant.

For weeks, Mirza had watched helplessly as the closest thing he had to a son slipped steadily into depression. Vikrant became a compulsive workaholic, his smoking went up almost three times and he started drinking simply so that he could sleep instead of lying awake in bed, thinking of her.

'You know the funniest part, sir?' a slurring Vikrant once said to Mirza on the phone at 4 in the morning. 'She's no longer with him, either. Apparently he's an asshole of the first order and she dumped him in two weeks.'

Shaina's deputation with the IB had ended by then and she was transferred to another location. Vikrant eventually realized that he was destroying himself and slowly brought his life back on track after six months. But he never let himself get close to anyone again, and hardly smiled after that. Most of his jokes were dark, and his chuckles were either at Mirza's exasperation at him or indicated something sinister.

And now, as the chopper took off from the Pawan Hans airbase in Juhu, Vikrant made it a point not to look at Shaina, who was seated in front of him. Also in the chopper were Usman Qureshi, Mazhar Khan, Shaukat Asad, and Mustafa and Ibrahim Kadir, otherwise known as the IM Five.

# 31

*Monday evening, Lakshadweep.*

It wasn't as if Mirza hadn't anticipated this. However, as he got off the chopper, he still found himself shaking his head at the chaos that lay ahead.

Mirza, Goyal and Jaiswal had followed Vikrant in another chopper towards an Indian Navy aircraft carrier, which was docked 50 nautical miles from the hijacked cruise liner, just off the coast of Kavaratti. The site of the INS *Dweeprakshak*, the Indian Navy base on Lakshadweep, Kavaratti is among the bigger and more important islands in Lakshadweep.

Mankame, against his wishes, had been asked to stay in Mumbai and work with the RAW team that was tracking the supposed autorickshaw driver. Before leaving, he had hugged Vikrant for a long minute at Pawan Hans.

'I never said thank you,' said Mankame. 'For saving my life that day.'

'Say it after I'm back,' Vikrant replied.

The aircraft carrier was buzzing with activity, carrying representatives from IB, RAW, the PMO and the navy. Minutes earlier, the chopper carrying Vikrant, Shaina and the IM Five had landed. The five terrorists were led to a lock-up on the lower level, while Vikrant and Shaina were huddled in a conference around a table in the Officers' Room.

'If we include the captain and his crew, there are a total of forty-eight hostages on board that cruise liner,' an IB officer was saying as Mirza entered. They turned and acknowledged him, and he motioned to them to get on with it, taking his place around the table next to Vikrant.

'There are twelve women, six teenagers and two kids under ten years, who will be our priority. We need to demand their release in exchange for the terrorists,' the officer continued.

'We're giving in?' Mirza asked.

'We're going to negotiate, of course,' the PMO representative, Akhilesh Kumar Mishra, said. 'But let's face it. They have almost fifty of our people, and they are docked near our naval base. If they have weapons with them, say a rocket launcher or a bomb, they could hurt us really badly.'

Mirza and Vikrant both turned around to look at the bureaucrat before exchanging looks with each other.

'Let's talk options,' the IB officer said. 'Say we have to storm the cruise liner. Is there a way to do it without letting the hostages come to any harm?'

'We could do a blitzkrieg,' Shaina said. 'Shoot enough flashbang grenades through the windows to disorient everyone for a minute and slip inside. With enough flashbangs and shooters, we could pull it off. The problem is, we don't have enough time to study the layout of the cruise liner, so we'll have to play it by ear.'

'Has anyone considered stealth?' the RAW officer said. 'Slip a team of marine commandoes inside somehow? Take the hijackers out one by one?'

'Again, too many unknowns,' the navy commander said. 'We have no idea where the terrorists are positioned.'

The room fell silent as everyone racked their brain. Then Vikrant spoke up.

'If you're all done,' he said, 'can we start being realistic?'

Everyone turned to him.

'You know a better way, Mr Singh?' the navy commander asked.

'There is no better or worse way,' Vikrant said. 'There is only one way. Let me take the five prisoners to that cruise liner. It is the only way to ensure that the hostages are freed. We can insist that they let the women and children go first, and the rest after I get on board with the five IM members. And let us not forget that even if we manage to get all the hostages released, there's still that small matter of the '93 Cache. Those five men have been in possession of some really serious arsenal and we have no idea what they've done with it.'

'And then what?' Mirza snapped. 'Watch as they shoot you?'

Vikrant turned to his mentor.

'Wrong time for you to start getting emotional, isn't it, sir?' he said. 'After an entire career of hard decisions?'

Mirza stormed out, followed by Vikrant, while the others in the room exchanged looks.

Thirty minutes later, Mirza was on the phone with Marco.

'I need a show of good faith before I give you what you want,' he said.

Marco laughed. 'We're a group of armed men holdin' civilians hostage and askin' for the release of five terrorists, Mr Mirza. Good faith ain't something you should be seekin' in this particular market. But sure, you can have some of your people back.'

The IM five were led up to the carrier's deck, where Vikrant was waiting for them, Mirza standing behind him. They stood in formation, Qureshi, their leader, standing in front, Shaukat Asad and Mazhar Khan on his left, and Mustafa and Ibrahim Kadri on his right. Their handcuffs were removed under the watchful eyes of fifteen naval soldiers who had their guns trained on them. Mustafa and Ibrahim stepped forward.

'Where's our mother?' Mustafa asked.

'Didn't you hear?' Vikrant said, injecting a good measure of insolence in his grin. 'She was driven out of her house.'

Mustafa moved towards Vikrant but Ibrahim pulled him back.

Across the water, Marco's men led twenty of the hostages up the deck and bundled them into two lifeboats at gunpoint. They were a mixed group: old men, women and children. The navy had set up powerful zoom cameras on the deck of the aircraft carrier, which were trained on the cruise liner and relaying a live feed to a screen in the Officers' Room. Everyone in there could see the fear on the hostages' faces.

Vikrant and the IM Five boarded another lifeboat. All three lifeboats were lowered into the water at the same time. Vikrant navigated the one he was in, while each lifeboat carrying the hostages was navigated by one of them. Vikrant's lifeboat passed between the two before reaching the cruise liner.

Mirza quickly made his way to the Officers' Room and joined the group staring at the screen. They watched as a rope ladder was lowered and Vikrant boarded the cruise liner, followed by the IM Five. The five terrorists were welcomed with handshakes by Marco and another hijacker, who was clearly Marco's second-in-command. Mustafa Kadri turned to Vikrant and said something.

'Please keep your bloody mouth shut, lad,' Mirza said softly even as Vikrant was seen responding. Mustafa punched him in the gut and Vikrant doubled over. Ibrahim came forward and kicked Vikrant as well, making him fall to the ground.

As Vikrant was dragged away to the lower level of the cruise liner, Shaina stifled a sob and Mirza, unseen by anyone, gave her hand a quick squeeze.

# 32

*Monday night, cruise liner.*

Daniel took a deep puff of his cigarette as he looked around the recreational area where they were being held.

Half an hour earlier, Marco had entered the area with his trademark smile.

'Good news,' he said. 'An exchange is happenin'. I need all women, children and old men to form a straight line near the door.'

Two of Marco's henchmen stepped forward, guns at the ready.

'These men will take you upstairs and before ya know it, y'all be aboard an Indian Navy vessel. So, please start comin' forward.'

Some of the hostages started shuffling around, unsure of whether to believe Marco.

Daniel and Hakimi stood up almost in tandem.

'May I?' Daniel asked Marco, gesturing at the hostages. The Somali nodded and Daniel went over to a woman, who had a four-year-old boy with her. Kneeling down, he started speaking softly to her, willing her to get up. Hakimi went over to another hostage and soon, twenty-five captives were standing in a line near the door.

Daniel went over to Vaishali, who shook her head, looking stubborn.

'Look—' he began.

'Shut up,' she said. 'I'm not leaving you.'

Daniel went closer to her. 'Listen to me,' he whispered urgently. 'Get to safety. That's one less thing for me to worry about.'

Before Vaishali could respond, Marco spoke. 'She stays,' he said. 'And so do you.'

Daniel turned around.

Marco then pointed to Hakimi. 'You can leave,' he said. Calmly, Hakimi strode up to Daniel and Vaishali and sat down with his back to the wall.

'I'm not leaving either,' he told Daniel, who looked helplessly from Hakimi to Vaishali.

'What's happenin', Mr Union Leader?' Marco called out from across the room.

'Nothing, sir,' Daniel said. 'That's all of them.'

Marco looked at Hakimi for a moment.

'Last chance,' he said.

Hakimi stared back coolly at Marco, neither speaking nor moving. Marco shrugged and turned around, leading the line of hostages out of the door.

The remaining passengers sat in silence for another half hour before the door slid open. Two of the Somali gunmen dragged in a man by his arms and shoved him to the ground. Marco entered a second later.

'Mr Union Leader,' he said, and Daniel stood up.

'This man is known to be somethin' of a rule-breaker. If he breaks any of my rules, I kill either the lady sittin' by your side or the brave old man next to her,' Marco said casually.

'Where did he come from, sir?' Daniel asked.

'None of your business, sir,' Marco replied before walking out, followed by his men. The door slid shut and the new entrant pulled himself to his feet slowly. Daniel walked over to him.

Both men stared at each other.

'Madman Dan,' Vikrant said after a few seconds.

'Toothpick Vik,' Daniel replied, with a surprised grin. Both men shook hands warmly.

'You two know each other?' Hakimi asked curiously.

'We've worked together. Vik here is with the National Investigation Agency, and one hell of an investigator.'

'And I don't know how well you know this man,' Vikrant said. 'But if there's one person I'd blindly trust with my life, it's Madman Dan Fernando.'

Vikrant and Daniel went to where Hakimi and Vaishali were sitting. The two remaining hostages, a man in his late thirties named Saahir Mastan and a girl in her early twenties, Prajakta Desai, instinctively drew closer to them too.

The night before they were supposed to call Marco, Mirza and his team had worked intensively to draw up a plan of action. Goyal and Jaiswal were asked to go through the list of hostages provided by the cruise company to see if there was anyone whose help Vikrant could potentially enlist once he was aboard.

'Here's one,' Goyal called out. 'Former Army Special Forces, Daniel Fernando.'

Both Mirza and Vikrant looked at Goyal, then at each other.

'Let me see that,' Vikrant said and took the list from Goyal. One look at Daniel's picture and Vikrant looked relieved.

'There is a God after all,' he said.

Five years ago, when Vikrant was in the final year of his IB stint, he had been sent on one of his most important missions. A deep cover secret agent in Pakistan had gone on the run after his cover was blown. He had managed to slip into Bangladesh undetected and needed help to get to India. The problem was that the ISI, suspecting he might do something like that, had already sent its own people to watch the Indo-Bangladesh border at Malda in West Bengal.

Vikrant was asked to leave for Malda and stay in contact with the agent, while the Army Special Forces provided assistance through Daniel.

In a makeshift command centre deep in the forest near the Indian side of the border, Vikrant would speak to the agent, who was hiding in a nearby village in Bangladesh, every half hour, and relay the information to Daniel.

'This isn't going to work till we get an idea of what we're up against, Vik,' Daniel told Vikrant over the radio on the second day.

'I know. But we don't have ground assets on the other side of the border at this moment,' Vikrant replied.

'Yes, you do,' said Daniel. 'I slipped across fifteen minutes ago.'

Daniel went off the line before an annoyed Vikrant could say anything. For the next hour, Vikrant paced about in the command centre. Finally, the radio crackled.

'Send help to the border, Vik,' Daniel hissed. 'Now.'

Vikrant went by his gut instinct and decided to trust Daniel. A team of armed BSF men waited at the Malda border as Daniel sped towards them in a stolen car. There were two other cars hot on his trail but they quickly lost interest on seeing the BSF. Daniel, armed only with a pistol and a dagger and dressed as a peasant, had singlehandedly taken out seven disguised ISI killers, rescued the IB agent, stolen a car and made it across.

'I see why they call you Madman Dan,' Vikrant later told Daniel over a drink.

'I'll take that as a compliment, Toothpick Vik,' Daniel responded.

'What?'

'Vic Vega? *Reservoir Dogs*?' Daniel asked.

Vikrant stared blankly.

Before they had parted ways, Daniel gifted Vikrant a DVD of the Quentin Tarantino movie.

Now, Vikrant and Daniel updated each other with what they knew while everyone else looked at them with renewed hope.

'We need to figure out a way to get some intel about this place to the people on the aircraft carrier,' Vikrant said.

'We already did.' Daniel smiled.

# 33

'What else can you tell us?' Mirza asked.

Aastha Sachdev stroked her four-year-old son's hair as he slept with his head on her lap, and thought hard.

The twenty hostages released by Marco and his men had been brought aboard the aircraft carrier by the navy and taken for a full medical check-up. Two of them, Aastha and a teenager, Gaurav Sanyal, had asked to speak to 'someone in charge' before they went for the check-up.

'It's really important,' Aastha said.

Shaina, who was helping the navy, overheard them and took them to see Mirza. Both hostages were now seated in a small room on the lower deck.

'Well, this dude Daniel was like, make sure they know the hostages being held in the rec area down below. And they've got these really badass sub-machine guns from Israel or somewhere, and some pistols,' Gaurav said.

153

Mirza turned to Shaina for help.

'Badass,' she said. 'It's slang. The latest word for impressive.' She turned to Gaurav.

'These sub-machine guns. Were they Uzis?' she asked and Gaurav nodded vigorously.

'And the pistols were ... clock?' he said, hesitantly.

'Glock?' she asked, and both Gaurav and Aastha nodded this time.

'They also have plenty of ammunition. The captain was up in the engine room most of the time, I think, to give the impression to the control room that everything was normal. Daniel said he counted twelve hijackers. And he felt that they were ex-soldiers because, you know, Daniel is one as well and he knows the type,' Aastha said.

'Daniel Fernando?' Mirza asked.

'Yeah. He just took over like a boss after we got hijacked. Stood up to those gunmen and shit. It was wicked. Him and the other old dude were, like, totally in control while the rest of us were losing our shit. The oldie even saved a woman from getting raped,' Gaurav gushed.

Aastha winced at the memory and Shaina turned to her.

'What is he talking about?' she asked.

'Well, one of the hijackers sneaked into the recreational area while we were sleeping. Tried to take away a young woman at gunpoint. This old man, we all called him Uncle, he just stood up to the hijacker, telling him to go ahead and shoot him, but he won't let the hijacker take the girl. We were all so terrified.' Aastha trembled at the memory.

Shaina put a hand on Aastha's shoulder to calm her down.

'So, to sum it up, there are fifteen men armed with Uzis and Glocks and plenty of ammunition. They seem to be trained ex-soldiers. The hostages are being held in the recreational area and are given meals twice a day. The captain was told to maintain the illusion that everything was normal till they were ready to reveal the hijack. Correct?'

'Yep, yep. Also, the army dude thinks there's a mole,' Gaurav chimed in.

Mirza stared at him hard before speaking.

'I want you to repeat that without using any slang,' he said.

'Okay, well … Daniel thinks that someone among the hostages might have been … on the side of the hijackers…'

'And why does he think that?'

Gaurav shrugged.

'IDK, man,' he said.

'WHAT?!!' Mirza now lost his cool.

'That … that means I don't know…' a startled Gaurav stammered. 'There wasn't much time. The dude … I mean Daniel just whispered this to me as I was leaving, saying that this was important.'

Shaina took Aastha and Gaurav away as Mirza sat alone, processing the information.

He then walked to the Officers' Room, where he drew Goyal and Jaiswal aside and told them to talk to all the released hostages about the 'uncle' who had stood up to the hijacker.

'You have a plan, sir?' Goyal asked.

'Just a thought,' Mirza replied. 'He might be a possible ally, and we need everyone we can get.'

Then Mirza walked out to the deck and used one of the phones to call Mankame.

'What's happening, boy?' he asked.

'We're still watching the autorickshaw driver, sir. He drove to a garage in Malad after leaving Behrambaug. Parked the auto there and drove out on a bike, dressed in different clothes. From there, he went to Goregaon and entered a residential building. It's a single-wing building, nothing fancy. Hasn't come out since.'

'See what you can find out, but be careful. And be ready to move in when I tell you to.'

Mirza ended the call and turned around just as Jaiswal came up behind him.

'It's Qureshi,' he said. 'He wants to speak to you.'

Mirza hurried to the Officers' Room, where the naval commander and several others were huddled around a phone which had its speakerphone light on.

'This is Mirza,' he said.

'Listen carefully, Mirza,' the leader of the IM Five said. 'I have taken over from Marco, which means that he and his team will do exactly as I ask. If you don't tell me where Mustafa and Ibrahim's mother is, I'll bring Vikrant up to the deck and torture him in front of those cameras you have pointed at us.'

'How is Vikrant?' Mirza asked.

'He's alive. Where is the old woman?'

Mirza hesitated for a second before replying, 'She's safe. We've put her up at a hotel in Bandra with three female cops for company.'

'You better not be lying,' Qureshi threatened.

'I have no reason to,' Mirza replied. 'The whole thing was done to draw you guys out anyway, which is pointless now.'

'Which hotel?'

Mirza told him.

'Good. I want her back at her home and speaking to me on this satellite phone in two hours.'

'Fine.'

'Next. There's a commercial freighter headed our way.'

Mirza exchanged looks with Jaiswal and Goyal.

'I want you to let it reach us unhindered. Anyone tries anything funny, a hostage dies.'

'What's on the freighter?' Mirza asked.

'Someone very important,' Qureshi responded and the line went dead.

For a minute, nobody spoke. Only Mirza, Goyal and Jaiswal looked at each other, all of them thinking the same thing.

*Munafiq.*

# 34

*Tuesday early morning, Mumbai.*

'Heads up,' Sonam Dhillon said into her mike.

Sonam, her men and DCP Ashok Mankame had split up into teams of three to watch the autorickshaw driver. Sonam and two of her colleagues kept an eye on the front entrance of the building in one car, while Mankame and the remaining two watched the rear, just in case their target tried to jump over the compound wall. The entire night the team members took turns to watch, one of them standing guard while the other two slept in the back seats of the cars.

Half an hour earlier, Mirza had called Sonam to tell her about his conversation with Qureshi and inform her that he was ordering the female cops to release Shagufta Bi. Sonam had woken up the sleeping officers and they had all taken positions along the Western Express Highway, assuming that the autorickshaw driver would find it the fastest route from the building in Goregaon to the hotel in Bandra.

Early in the morning, he had left on his bike and Sonam had given him a five-minute lead before pulling out into the street. The IB officers' main concern was that the man might identify a tail, because traffic wasn't too thick on the highway that early in the morning. Mankame was asked to rush to the hotel so that he could keep an eye on Shagufta Bi as she came out. As the autorickshaw driver pulled onto the highway, Mankame called up Sonam to tell her that he would be at the hotel in ten minutes. Sonam said a little prayer of thanks and sped past her target as one of her teammates replaced her as the tail.

In half an hour, the man was pulling up outside the hotel where Shagufta Bi was waiting with the policewomen. They bid her adieu and one of them even hugged her as they helped her onto the back seat. When the biker started driving towards Jogeshwari, the morning traffic had begun thickening and Mankame smoothly slipped into the stream of vehicles while two others sped ahead, ready to take turns.

They played the game all the way up to Behrambaug, where Mankame parked his SUV on the main road and walked to the Kadir residence, just in time to see the man waving goodbye to Shagufta Bi before turning his bike around. Mankame walked past the house without slowing down and rounded a corner, after which he called Sonam and updated her. He waited for a good ten minutes before jogging back to the main road and getting into his SUV.

Halfway to Goregaon, he received a call from Sonam and answered using his hands-free.

'Just heard from our surveillance guys,' she told him. 'Shagufta Bi made a call to a satellite phone located in Lakshadweep. Spoke for five minutes to both her sons.'

'Showtime?' Mankame asked.

'Showtime.'

Mankame pressed the accelerator and turned on his siren, causing vehicles ahead of him to slowly, reluctantly give him way.

He could see the biker up ahead, while the RAW members, in their own vehicles, were slowly closing in on him. Sonam pulled up in front of the target, boxing him in, and the entire cluster of vehicles came to a halt in the middle of the Western Express Highway.

Mankame and Sonam sprang out of their cars, guns drawn, while Awasthi caught the man by the neck and dragged him off the bike straight into Mankame's SUV. Mankame handcuffed the man and pushed him inside, and Sonam and Awasthi got in on either side. Climbing into the driver's seat, Mankame sped away as the rest of the IB team cleared their vehicles as well as the target's bike off the road amidst the impatient honking by waiting cars.

Ten minutes later, Mankame brought the SUV to a screeching halt outside the Crime Branch Unit X office in Andheri. The man, who had on route identified himself as Wasim, was dragged inside the unit office and brought straight to an interrogation room.

For the first ten minutes, no one asked Wasim anything. Two of Mankame's burliest and most experienced constables rained blows on him as he cried out in pain, while the DCP, Sonam and Awasthi just sat on stools in a corner, watching.

The constables paused for breath as Wasim writhed on the ground. Mankame went over to him, a cigarette dangling from his mouth, and knelt down.

'They can go on,' he told Wasim. 'All day. And then we'll move on to some more creative methods.'

'What … what do you want to know?' Wasim asked tearfully.

Mankame asked a third constable with a kinder face to take Wasim to the bathroom and get him cleaned up before bringing him to the cabin of the inspector in charge of the unit. When Wasim entered the cabin ten minutes later, there was tea waiting for him.

Wasim sat down shakily and poked at the teacup, half expecting to be beaten up again. When nothing happened, he took a sip gratefully.

'Who hired you?' Sonam asked.

'He said his name is Rishabh Chawla,' Wasim said.

Mankame leaned forward in his seat.

'Really?' he said.

Wasim nodded.

'He gave me a set of keys and a cellphone. Told me that he was heading out of the country for a few days and needed me to take care of some things. Paid me Rs 50,000 in cash and promised me more after he returned.'

'What else did he tell you?' Awasthi asked.

'That one of his men would call me. And that I should do exactly as they say and not ask any questions.'

Mankame held up a set of keys that he had seized, along with a cellphone and some cash, from Wasim's pockets after picking him up on the highway.

'Are these the keys he gave you?' he asked and Wasim nodded.

'One of them is for the bike. It was waiting for me at a garage in Malad.'

'The same one where you left the autorickshaw?' Sonam queried. They were firing questions from all sides to keep Wasim confused and docile.

Wasim looked startled but nodded.

'What are the other two for?'

'The house I'm staying in. One for the lock and one for the latch.'

'That's not your place?' Awasthi asked.

'I'm an auto driver, saheb. I can't afford a two-bedroom house. I stay in Kurla but was asked to stay in the Goregaon flat till I was told otherwise. Apparently, the owner had spoken to the watchman and a couple of neighbours. No one was surprised to see me.'

'Where is the owner?' said Mankame.

'No idea, sir. I have never even spoken to him.'

Mankame stood up and leaned over Wasim.

'If you're lying to me...'

'I'm not, sir. I only dealt with this Chawla.'

'You know the owner's name?' Mankame asked.

Wasim nodded.

# 35

**Tuesday afternoon, Lakshadweep.**

'I'm telling you, it's madness,' Hakimi said, struggling to keep his voice low.

'We're just discussing, uncle. Hypothetically. Let's just go with the flow,' Daniel said softly and Hakimi shook his head in exasperation.

'So,' Vikrant resumed, keeping his voice low. 'Say we can overpower the ones outside the door. That's two guards. Which means two Uzis, two Glocks and plenty of ammo. Plus two stiletto daggers.'

'Yes, but Marco sends a couple of others for a random check a couple of times in a day. I've seen their silhouettes behind the door in the afternoons. Also, one more person makes an inspection at least once a day. I've heard footsteps. And there's no fixed time for that. Which means that someone could walk in on us while we're overpowering the two,' Daniel said.

Hakimi, Daniel and Vikrant were huddled in a corner, while Vaishali kept the other two, Saahir and Prajakta, company.

'Say we get lucky,' Vikrant said and Hakimi shook his head again.

'Just suppose we get lucky,' Vikrant repeated earnestly before turning to Daniel. 'Can you lead the way to the top deck?'

Daniel nodded.

'It's pretty simple to traverse, but we'll have to be careful. They could be anywhere. Around any corner. At the first sound of gunfire, they'll come rushing downstairs. Which would have otherwise been fine, but we're going to have civilians in tow who might get hit by a stray bullet.'

'Stealth and silence are our best options,' Vikrant concurred. 'I say we use the daggers as far as possible.'

'How can you two even discuss this?' Hakimi hissed. 'You said that five men came aboard with you. That's sixteen men in all to deal with. Against the two of you. With all of us tagging behind. And who knows how many more are coming aboard?'

Daniel and Vikrant had different thoughts on this, but held back. Daniel was thinking about the possible mole on board, either among the guests or the crew. He had only whispered it to Gaurav as he was leaving, but had not told anyone else, not even Vikrant, because of his inherent tendency to not trust easily.

Vikrant, meanwhile, was thinking of the '93 Cache. He had no idea if Mirza or the others had found out anything more about it, but was pretty sure that the cache had been put to some very bad use. His primary fear was that if they tried to break out, one of the IM Five might detonate a bomb in Mumbai by simply dialling a number. Like Daniel, he, too, didn't trust people, and he did not want to add to the hostages' fear and panic, which was why he had not said anything about it even to Daniel.

The door slid open and two kitchen staff members came in, carrying packed sandwiches and milkshakes in plastic glasses. Earlier, they would hand out the refreshments to the hostages. This time, though, they simply placed the trays on the ground and walked out, followed by the guards within the minute.

Daniel and Vikrant looked at each other with a sinking feeling. The time was too short for a surprise attack.

Morosely, they started eating, both trying hard to think of an alternative plan. Hakimi went over to sit with Vaishali and the others, leaving them alone.

'Where's the captain?' Vikrant asked between bites. 'Sahani, right?'

Daniel nodded.

'They've mostly been keeping him and the crew in the engine room. Before they destroyed the radio, they needed him to keep in touch with land and give the impression that everything...'

Daniel trailed off and Vikrant looked at him.

'What?' Vikrant asked.

Daniel looked around to make sure that no one was within earshot.

'I suspect that we have a mole among us,' he said in a low voice. 'The way they took over the cruise liner within three hours was too smooth. They had to have had inside help.'

Vikrant's face changed.

'Sahani...' he said.

Daniel nodded and looked around once again before he went on.

'Maybe he was needed in the engine room earlier. But now, when the hijackers have contacted the government and the cruise liner is at a standstill, why are Sahani and his crew not here with us?'

'You think...'

'Perfect, right?' Daniel asked. 'He knows the cruise liner inside out.'

Vikrant was thinking hard.

'He doesn't even have to be one of them. He could have been pressurized in some way,' he said and told Daniel about Aslam Parkar.

'This is definitely ISI,' Daniel said and Vikrant nodded.

'There is a 1 per cent chance that Sahani is genuinely needed up in the engine room for something that they have planned. Maybe they're keeping the guests and the crew separate to thin our ranks or something,' Vikrant mused.

'Yes,' Daniel said. 'But only a 1 per cent chance.'

'And if the captain of the cruise liner, who knows every little thing about it, is with the enemy...' said Vikrant.

'Then we're at a huge tactical disadvantage,' Daniel finished.

# 36

The freighter eased slowly past the aircraft carrier, with ten naval guns pointed at it, and made its way towards the cruise liner.

At the forward end of the deck was a man dressed in black combat fatigues, with a black mask covering his head and face and an M4 assault rifle slung around his shoulder. He was standing with one leg on the railing, and coolly looked at the people gathered on the aircraft carrier's deck as he passed. He even gave a small salute to Mirza.

'Do you think it's him?' Goyal whispered.

'Too hard to tell. The build is right, but I need to see the face,' Mirza replied.

The freighter passed around the cruise liner and came to a halt parallel to it, standing between the cruise liner and Kavaratti island, going out of sight of the officers on the aircraft carrier. Two minutes later, the man in black fatigues went

167

aboard the cruise liner with the aid of a rope. Mirza entered the Officers' Room just in time to see him captured by the camera clambering on the top deck.

Qureshi came forward to greet him. They hugged and the man patted his back. Then Qureshi handed him the satellite phone. They watched as he dialled and three seconds later, the phone in the Officers' Room started ringing.

The naval commander put the call on speakerphone.

'I want to speak to Shahwaz Ali Mirza,' the caller said in a deep, guttural voice.

All eyes turned to the veteran spy, who just cleared his throat and said, 'I'm here.'

'Mirza,' the man said. 'Good to see you.'

'Have we met before?' Mirza said.

'Oh, we have. Lots of times. You just didn't realize it. Don't worry, though. This will soon be over and you will have your answers.'

'What do you want?'

'A journalist and a cameraman, with a live uplink.'

The room went silent.

'What?' Mirza finally asked.

'We want to go on TV, Mirza. Live.'

'What are you going to say?'

The man laughed.

'Come on,' he said. 'You never heard of freedom of the press?'

'Get serious,' Mirza growled.

'You want to get serious? Sure. How about this – get me a television news crew within an hour. If you do, I'll release some hostages. If you don't, I'll kill some. Is that clear?'

'Give me some hostages first,' Mirza said and there was an audible gasp around the room.

'What did you say?'

'We are bound to obey you because you are holding our people hostage. You, on the other hand, are not. I need to see some positive gesture on your part that I can use as a basis to get my government to agree to your demand.'

'I think you'll find your government more than willing to agree to my demand. But sure, I'll release the kitchen crew. I brought some supplies with me, so I don't think we'll be needing food any more.'

Mirza glanced at the screen and saw Qureshi and the others hauling cartons up to the cruise liner.

'This works the same way as earlier. You send a lifeboat with the news crew on board, I send a lifeboat with the kitchen staff. Anything else?'

'What's your name?' Mirza asked.

There was a chuckle.

'I have been called by many names. But you can call me Marwan.'

The line went dead and everyone in the Officers' Room looked at each other for a while.

Mirza turned to the PMO man, Akhilesh Mishra.

'Talk to the PM,' he said. 'Get it done.'

'Isn't that too much of a risk?' Mishra asked.

Mirza sighed heavily and stepped forward, coming close to him.

'I'm really trying to be patient with you, sir,' he said. 'I'd urge you not to test me. Do what you do, and let me do what I do. Please, talk to the PM.'

Without waiting for an answer, Mirza turned and walked away, beckoning Jaiswal and Goyal to follow him. As the three men left the room, Shaina turned to Mishra.

'I'd do as he says if I were you,' she told him.

It took more than an hour but at the end of it, a fighter jet carrying a reporter and a cameraman from a leading English news channel was on its way to the aircraft carrier.

'The channel's going to be touting this already,' said Mirza sourly. 'Exclusive. Explosive. Keep watching. It's going to be a circus.'

'PMO's going to be besieged,' Jaiswal mused.

'You seem distracted,' Goyal said to Mirza.

'Well, he does have a lot on his mind,' Jaiswal said sardonically and Goyal scowled.

He was about to respond but Mirza spoke first.

'Any of you feel that these hijackers are being too cooperative?' he asked.

Both his underlings looked at him expectantly.

'First, they let the oldies, women, kids and even some of the men go. Now they're giving us the kitchen staff.'

'Isn't … isn't that a good thing, sir?' Jaiswal asked uncertainly.

'For us, yes. But they're decreasing the number of hostages they have. With each move, they are left with fewer hostages for them to use and for us to worry about.'

'Well, they still have the captain and his crew, plus four civilians, Daniel Fernando and Vikrant sir,' said Goyal.

'Vikrant and Daniel could do some serious damage by themselves, and if the captain and his crew join them…'

Goyal and Jaiswal agreed.

'You think there's something else going on?' Goyal asked.

'I think there's a lot else going on. I think they're not depending simply on the hostages, that they have some ace up their sleeve that none of us know about.'

'Is there something you want us to do?' Jaiswal asked.

Mirza leaned back in his seat, thinking hard.

'Remember what we did while looking for the IM Five?' he said.

'We looked backwards?' Goyal asked.

Mirza nodded.

'It didn't get us any closer to the five bastards, but at least it unearthed a dual-faced shapeshifter.'

'You want to do that again?'

'We've hardly had any time to take a proper look at this mess since it started,' said Mirza. 'It's time to find out what we're missing.'

# 37

*Tuesday evening, Lakshadweep.*

It had taken the government an hour to decide, but in the end, three IB officers told the PMO that they couldn't pick anyone better than Sanjay Anand for the job.

Employed with one of the leading television news channels in India, Anand had started out as a crime reporter in Delhi twenty years ago and had climbed up the ranks to become one of the best journalists covering Islamic terrorism. His reports were thoroughly researched and, more importantly, balanced. He was among the few reporters who had not given in to the mass hysteria that television news peddled on a nationwide scale, instead choosing to quietly dish out meaningful and fair reportage. He had fearlessly visited war-torn regions across the country and had also been sent to the Middle East on several occasions, and not once had he displayed any sign of bias in his news reports.

The PMO contacted Anand's channel and struck a deal. Till the time Anand actually set foot on the hijacked cruise liner, the channel wouldn't give out any hint of what they were about to show. The editor, who was prone to get excited at the mere mention of an exclusive, threw a fit but ultimately agreed.

Anand and a cameraman were driven to the Palam Air Force Station in Delhi, where they were put aboard a fighter jet and flown to the aircraft carrier. There, they had a brief meeting with Mirza, after which Mirza called up Marwan and told him that they were ready. The journalist and his cameraman set off towards the cruise liner in a lifeboat, while the kitchen crew were lowered into the sea in another.

On boarding the cruise liner, Anand and his cameraman were subjected to a body search, after which they were led to the open-air cafeteria, where Marwan sat, his M4 resting casually across his legs. The camera on the aircraft carrier was zoomed in on the cafeteria as Anand was offered a seat across from Marwan, while his cameraman set up his equipment.

Part of the PMO's deal with Anand's employers was that a direct uplink be provided to the aircraft carrier so that the interview could be viewed live by everyone in the Officers' Room as well.

As everyone involved had anticipated, the interview with Marwan sparked off instant panic in two places – Mumbai and Lakshadweep.

Mumbai, because the first thing Marwan said to Anand was, 'Mumbai is under threat. From us.'

In the Officers' Room, everyone winced. The cat was officially out of the bag.

'Only we know where the attack will happen. But suffice to say we have everything, from arms to explosives to men who are very, very committed to our cause, and can be put to use the minute I say the word,' Marwan continued.

After a second's pause, Anand's voice was heard off-screen. Despite what Marwan had just said, there was no sign of fear in his voice.

'And what is your cause?' he asked.

Marwan's reply was tinged with scorn.

'What has it always been? The Universal Caliphate. The world has always been ours for the taking, and we are going to take it, no matter how many attempts are made by infidels to stop us.'

'You're going to establish the Universal Caliphate from a cruise liner in the Arabian Sea?' Anand asked sardonically.

Everyone in the Officers' Room froze a little, with the exception of Mirza. On the cruise liner, Marwan sniggered audibly under his mask.

'I am just doing my part, the way millions like me are, across the world. But I understand your curiosity. Greater minds than yours have made the plan that is now unfolding in front of you. I do not expect you to comprehend it,' he said.

'So, you're saying that you will slaughter countless people in Mumbai unless we give in to your demands?'

'Slaughter is necessary, Mr Anand. Nothing comes without sacrifice. And I'm sure, after you hear what I have in mind, you will realize that holding an entire city to ransom is justified.'

'A lot of people will have a problem with your use of the word "justified". But I'm sure you know that already.'

Marwan nodded.

'I do. And I do not have time to argue with you.'

'So what do you want?' Anand asked.

Marwan leaned forward in his seat.

'Lakshadweep.'

# 38

*Tuesday evening, Lakshadweep.*

There was silence in the Officers' Room.

There was silence in the newsroom of the television channel in Delhi, where the interview was being broadcast live.

There was silence in the Prime Minister's Office, where the PM and around fifty others were glued to the television set.

There was silence at the IB headquarters, where everyone from the IB chief downwards was watching the interview.

There was silence in countless offices of law enforcement agencies across India, as well as in the offices of intelligence agencies in at least four countries that had been informed of the situation as part of international cooperation. In every house, office or store where the interview was being watched, there was nothing but puzzled silence at Marwan's demand. People in Mumbai, who had been in the initial throes of panic after listening to Marwan's threat, were frozen into bewilderment.

Marwan, seemingly aware of the reaction he was going to evoke, sat back and waited for Anand to respond. Anand gathered himself after more than half a minute and said, 'Would you like to elaborate on that?'

'Gladly. We want Lakshadweep for ourselves. As a separate state. As part of the Universal Caliphate. And if the islands of Lakshadweep are not handed over to us within twenty-four hours, Mumbai will burn.'

'Were you anticipating this?' Goyal asked in a low voice.

Mirza only shook his head as he, Goyal and Jaiswal walked out of the Officers' Room.

The rest of the interview seemed anti-climactic after the shocker that Marwan dropped with his demand for Lakshadweep. Anand asked him if he thought that the people of Lakshadweep would accept his demand. Marwan chuckled.

'This is a question that you should be asking them, not me,' he said.

Mirza did not think that the population of Lakshadweep would want to be separated from India. In 1947, the population of Lakshadweep, which is now over 90 per cent Muslim, was almost 100 per cent Muslim. As the cluster of islands was cut off from the rest of the country at the time, the people there did not learn about India's independence till a few days after 15 August. Sardar Vallabhbhai Patel, after being appointed union home minister, had sent an Indian Navy frigate to keep an eye on the islands in case Pakistan tried claiming it.

It is said that Pakistani Navy vessels had indeed been spotted heading towards Lakshadweep a few days after Independence, but the presence of the Indian Navy frigate and the Indian flag hoisted high on the island, discouraged any attempt at a takeover.

But more importantly, Mirza thought, there had been no demand from the natives for separation, unlike in states such as Punjab where the people wanted to be part of a separate state. Pakistan, at the time, had counted on the Muslim-majority population in Lakshadweep supporting their demand but the idea did not find any takers in the people themselves.

But it wasn't 1947 any more. A lot of water had passed under the bridge, so to speak. Many incidents had swayed the opinion of Muslims not just in India, but the world over. The sheer number of 'recruits' for the cause of the Global Caliphate seen every year was testament to the change in thinking due to attacks by Islamic terrorists and the backlash that the Muslim community faced, which, in turn, became fuel for extremists to use in their propaganda.

The interview ended with Marwan saying that for the next twenty-four hours, he did not want anyone entering or exiting Lakshadweep. For a minute, everyone on the aircraft carrier was worried that he might kill Anand on live television. However, the journalist was allowed to leave and everyone heaved a collective sigh of relief when he clambered aboard the aircraft carrier. He was sent packing in a jet before he could ask the officers any questions.

Mirza walked to the room that he had taken over for himself to take a closer look at the entire incident. He, along with Goyal and Jaiswal, was slowly piecing together the entire run-up to the hijacking.

'Let's go over it again,' Mirza said.

'Okay. So, Munafiq first gets to Aslam Parkar. Holding him and his mother captive in their house, he poses as Rishabh Chawla and appears for the IM Five in Bhopal. He relays instructions for them to break out of jail while also making all arrangements for them once they are out,' Jaiswal said.

'Right,' Goyal picked it up. 'The IM Five collect the '93 Cache from wherever it was hidden and do God knows what with it. Then they shave off their beards, get different hairstyles, put on posh suits and check into the Taj Land's End.'

Mirza said nothing. He was sitting back in his chair, pinching the bridge of his nose with one hand, eyes closed, listening to his two subordinates.

'Meanwhile, Marco hijacks the cruise liner and waits for orders. He was waiting till the IM Five had used the '93 Cache for their purpose, before moving forward. Do we agree on that?'

'It's the most logical explanation,' Mirza said without opening his eyes.

'Okay. So once the IM Five are done with their stuff, they let their masters know. Marco goes ahead with contacting our government and Marwan sets off from Indonesia for Lakshadweep,' said Jaiswal.

'Which brings us here,' Goyal added.

'What are the questions we need answered?' Mirza asked.

There was a minute's silence as Goyal and Jaiswal marshalled their thoughts.

'Well, how do they propose to keep Lakshadweep under their control? There are too many challenges. They don't know if the people will agree. Ruling by force never ends well. Plus, our navy could take it back from them in a day,' Goyal said.

'Yes, but at the cost of a lot of lives. Are we sure we'd want to go that way?' Mirza asked.

'Well,' Jaiswal said. 'I guess that's something the government can answer. Meanwhile, here's another question. What's on that freighter? The one that Marwan came on? It's been standing between the cruise liner and Kavaratti and we haven't seen any movement on it.'

'Can't we slip someone on board, somehow?' Goyal wondered and Mirza shook his head.

'Too risky,' he said.

'Next, can we trust this Daniel Fernando?' asked Jaiswal.

'I believe we can,' Mirza replied. 'I've gone over his record and there is nothing in there to indicate that he's anything but dependable. He's also worked on covert operations earlier, and Vikrant and he have worked together. So, yes, we can trust him.'

'Good. Because I'm beginning to think Vikrant sir and he are the only ones in the position to actually do something, while we sit here and scratch our heads.'

'Patience, lad,' Mirza said.

'Okay, one big question. Do we think Marwan is Munafiq?' Goyal asked.

'That's a big one,' Mirza said. 'Every attack that he's been part of, or orchestrated, he's always made sure that he's been present at the scene. This time, we're in the middle of the sea. The media is banned from coming close. The only ones near enough to actually see what's going on are us, the people on Lakshadweep and the people on the cruise liner.'

Everyone looked at each other.

'So, Munafiq could be Marwan?' Jaiswal said.

'He could be. But then again, he might not be.'

Goyal and Jaiswal looked confused.

'Munafiq has always remained in the shadows. It's not his style to come out in the open and assume charge of an operation with everyone watching him,' Mirza said thoughtfully.

'But if Marwan isn't Munafiq, then where is Munafiq? Why is he missing out on the fruition of his plan, which he's worked so hard on?' Goyal countered.

'What if this isn't the fruition?' Mirza asked.

'Oh please, don't tell me this nightmare is going to last longer,' Jaiswal groaned.

Mirza took a deep breath and stood up. He started pacing about the small room.

'This story began in Bhopal. It went to Mumbai and then came to Lakshadweep. And it sure as hell isn't going to end with the Island of Lakshadweep being handed over to Marwan on a platter. Whatever they have planned, it involves hitting us hard. In tangible terms. They have to shed blood and take lives.'

'What are you saying, sir?' Goyal asked.

'That we might still see another chapter in this story. And that Munafiq may already be in that location.'

# 39

*Wednesday morning, Mumbai/Lakshadweep.*

It did not take more than a few hours for mass hysteria to set in.

The press reacted the fastest, as expected. Crime reporters reached out to their sources in the police and investigative agencies and were told that the matter was being handled by the higher-ups. Mumbai Police Commissioner Virendra Sinha met journalists for five minutes in his office, in which all he said was that he was under orders not to speak to the media, and that the Chief Minister's Office would be in a better position to comment.

As they walked out after the press briefing, the crime reporters called up their colleagues on the political beat, who laid siege to the Chief Minister's Office. CM Yashwant Pradhan, after frantic phone calls to Delhi, stepped out to address the media.

For the next half hour, he fielded questions from journalists who were all but frothing at the mouth. Pradhan could not outright deny what Marwan had said on live television. If the people of Mumbai were in danger, they had a right to know. At the same time, he did not want to set off any extreme reactions.

That decision, however, was taken out of his hands the minute the press briefing ended. The press, predictably, went crazy. It began with live reports from outside the Mantralaya. Soon, reporters were covering search-and-combing operations by the police all over the city. The entire NSG hub in Goregaon was put on standby and journalists stationed themselves outside, giving hourly bulletins that didn't actually say anything new but added to the mass hysteria.

Before long, people were packing whatever they could and bundling it into their cars. That is, those who had cars. Taxis and autorickshaws were unavailable, as the drivers were busy getting themselves out of the city. Within a couple of hours, highways leading out of the city were jammed with vehicles.

The police set up roadblocks and random checkpoints on orders from the commissioner, further adding to the chaos. Everyone was scared, even the policemen, who were doing their jobs while others fled. Pradhan was scared. The state cabinet was scared. The union government was scared.

In Lakshadweep, meanwhile, a different sort of reaction was brewing. The residents of the islands had noticed the cruise liner anchored near Kavaratti and had been curiously keeping an eye on it. Then the naval aircraft carrier arrived, followed by the freighter. When some of the locals tried to take their boats out to take a closer look, the INS *Dweeprakshak* sent naval ships to turn them back. Instructions were issued to the residents to stay indoors until further notice.

Then came the interview with Marwan. As soon as it ended, residents poured out into the streets on all ten islands of Lakshadweep. The navy deployed heavy personnel immediately. It took a couple of hours but the naval officers were able to convince the locals that the best thing they could do at the moment was to stay indoors and not panic.

Prime Minister Parmeshwar Naidu, meanwhile, called up the administrator of Lakshadweep, Danish Khan.

'What am I to tell my people, sir?' Khan asked.

'Danish,' Naidu said. 'We've known each other for two decades now. Trust me, I'll find a way.'

'I'm not surrendering Lakshadweep to these barbarians, sir.'

'You won't have to, Danish,' Naidu assured him and hung up with absolutely no idea of what he was going to do next.

From the deck of the cruise liner, Marwan watched the developments on Lakshadweep using binoculars and smiled to himself. Everything was going perfectly in accordance with the plan.

# 40

*Wednesday morning, Lakshadweep.*

After Marwan reached the hijack site in his freighter, the Somali mercenaries transferred crates full of supplies, including drinking water and tinned food, to the cruise liner. This was to sustain them as well as their captives till they received the order to move on to the next phase of the mission.

'And what would the next phase be?' Marco asked.

'All in good time, Marco,' Marwan said from under his mask. 'All in good time.'

Marco assigned two of his men to take food and water twice a day to the recreational area of the cruiser, where the six captives were being held. The supplies were stored in the kitchen, and every morning and evening, one of them would load a tray and take it down to the captives.

Today, the job was assigned to Oscar, who started his trip from the kitchen to the recreational area with a sense of supreme boredom. Agreed, he thought, it was easy money. The captives had been obedient and no one had tried being a hero, although Marco had told him to keep a close eye on the man who was playing union leader.

For the most part, Oscar thought as he started down the staircase, he was basically babysitting a bunch of people and getting paid for it. Which, though not a bad thing, was boring. He had spent years in battle zones all around the world, and this, while easy, also came with the lack of action that could affect any battle-hardened veteran.

He nodded to two of his fellow mercenaries who were standing lazily a short distance away from the doors, guns to their sides, chatting with each other. Strictly speaking, they were supposed to be stationed on either side of the doors. But as the days passed, they had started slacking off in increasing degrees. Oscar couldn't blame them. The job was monotonous and in any case there were just six unarmed people, two of them women, to guard. There was only one way out of the recreational area and anyone trying to escape would quickly be brought down by bullets before they could take five steps.

Inside the recreational area, Vikrant and Daniel, observing the silhouettes of the guards through the translucent doors, had also picked up on their pattern of movements and had based their plans around it, despite Hakimi's protests.

'Now,' Daniel whispered as he saw Oscar's silhouette approach. Vikrant flicked the cigarette lighter in his hand.

The walls of the recreational area were lined with canvas paintings about the history of sailing and maritime trade, all in wooden frames. From early that morning, Daniel and Vikrant had pulled every painting off the walls and gathered them in the middle. The plan was risky as hell, perfectly in keeping with Madman Dan.

Vikrant touched the flame of the lighter to the heap of paintings and it caught fire instantly. By the time Oscar slid open one of the two sliding doors to the recreational area, the heap, which Daniel and Vikrant had placed just outside the door, was blazing in full force.

'What the fuck!' Oscar said, dropping the tray and going for his gun. He was one second too late. Daniel, who was crouching just beyond the door on Oscar's right, reached out and grabbed the stiletto dagger that Oscar was carrying in his boot holster. While Oscar, blinded by the smoke of the fire, was still reaching for the gun hanging by his side, Daniel drove the dagger into his jugular vein.

The two guards, alerted by Oscar's cry and the smell of fire, started running to the door. Daniel, without missing a beat, pulled out the same dagger and threw it at them, catching one in his left eye. He fell onto his fellow mercenary behind him and Vikrant, taking advantage of the confusion, ran forward.

'Don't try to wrestle them,' Daniel had told Vikrant. 'They're better trained, stronger and faster than you. Kill them the first chance you get.'

Vikrant did as he had been told. Pulling the dagger out of the fallen mercenary's eye, he pounced on the other one just as he was struggling to get up. With all the force that he could muster, Vikrant drove the dagger into the Somali's thorax. The mercenary clawed at Vikrant's face but Vikrant kept pushing the dagger till he stopped moving.

Daniel came up behind Vikrant and together, they pulled both the bodies inside. The previous night, all of them had filled every bucket and bottle they could find with water. As Vikrant and Daniel slid the doors shut, Hakimi, Vaishali, Saahir and Prajakta poured all the water on the fire, dousing it in perfect coordination.

Daniel stripped Oscar of his guns and ammunition and Vikrant did the same with one of the two others. They then went over to the body of the third mercenary and divided his ammunition between the two of them.

'Watch out!' Vaishali shouted, and Daniel and Vikrant looked up to see silhouettes of two more men advancing towards the door. It was a chance they had had to take. While there were only two guards on the level of the recreational area, the others were spread throughout the cruise liner and some of them were bound to be close enough to sense that something was amiss. Daniel and Vikrant had decided that they would play it by ear.

One of the two doors started sliding open and Daniel fired, shooting the mercenary through the door. He shot the other one, whose silhouette was clearly visible, too.

Moving quickly, Daniel passed the third mercenary's pistol to Hakimi. 'Just in case,' he told the old man and they all got into the formation that they had practised over and over the previous night.

Daniel and Vikrant were in front, Saahir and Hakimi behind them and Vaishali and Prajakta in the rear. Vaishali had protested at being placed in the back, saying that she wanted to play a more active part, but in the end she conceded to collective reasoning by Daniel, Hakimi and Vikrant.

'Move out!' Daniel commanded. Vikrant glanced at him. It was as if Madman Dan was back in the battlefield.

Vikrant slid the door open and they moved out together slowly. Both men kept their eyes peeled for the slightest movement, fingers on the triggers of their Uzis.

'How many more?' Vikrant asked Daniel.

'Five down. That leaves six Somalis and those five IM fucks,' Daniel said through gritted teeth as he and Vikrant collected ammunition from the two newly killed henchmen before moving forward.

They advanced along the corridor and reached the staircase just as three mercenaries appeared at the top of the stairs. Daniel and Vikrant both opened fire simultaneously and all the three went down.

'Fuck, that was lucky,' Vikrant said.

'Eight to go,' Daniel responded as he and Vikrant took positions on either side of the stairway. Hakimi and the others gathered behind Daniel.

Suddenly, in the doorway at the top of the stairs there appeared a tall, stocky figure wearing black combat fatigues and a black mask, holding an M4 assault rifle, with a bald, muscular Somali behind him.

'Who the hell is that?' Daniel asked.

'I have no clue,' Vikrant said, puzzled, taking a peek from behind his cover.

'Vikrant, Fernando,' the masked man said in a deep voice. 'If I'm guessing right, you are the ones leading this little adventure.'

Vikrant and Daniel exchanged glances.

'I'm giving you ten seconds to lay down your weapons and surrender. If you don't, what follows is on your head.'

The hostages could almost hear the seconds ticking by. Although Daniel and Vikrant had discussed such a situation the previous night, neither of them had been able figure out the best way to respond if they found themselves cornered and had decided to just go with the flow.

As the seconds passed, both looked at each other and shook their heads, almost at the same time, signifying no surrender. They reloaded their weapons and waited.

'Are you sure about this?' the man in black asked. No one said anything.

'Fine,' the deep voice said, this time a bit louder. 'I guess it's time, Abba.'

Daniel and Vikrant looked at each other, confused. Just then two shots rang out behind Daniel. He whirled around, his Uzi raised, and saw Hakimi standing behind Vaishali, his gun pressed to her temple. Saahir and Prajakta were lying on the floor, both bleeding from single gunshot wounds to their heads. Daniel could tell that they were already dead.

'Weapons down, boys,' Hakimi said calmly, pressing the gun harder against a terrified Vaishali's head. 'Marwan, beta, come on down.'

# 41

*Wednesday morning, Lakshadweep.*

Mirza, Jaiswal and Goyal were sprawled out on chairs, getting some much-needed sleep. None of them had slept for more than an hour after landing on the aircraft carrier. After reconstructing the events leading up to the demand for Lakshadweep, Mirza had insisted that they rest for a bit.

'Dropping dead from exertion isn't going to help anyone,' Mirza told Jaiswal and Goyal firmly, and made them put away their files.

They were woken up at dawn by Shaina's knocking on the door. She gave Mirza a satellite phone.

'DCP Mankame from Mumbai for you, sir,' she said. Mirza immediately shook himself awake and took the phone.

'Please tell me you've found the bloody '93 Cache,' Mirza said as Shaina left the room.

'How I wish, sir,' Mankame said. 'But there have been some developments you need to know about.'

'Tell me.'

'Well, Phadke called.'

'Who?' Mirza said, struggling to clear the cobwebs from his head.

'Senior Inspector Ravikant Phadke from Pune. The one we're working with on the Aslam Parkar angle.'

Mirza sat up.

'Keep talking.'

'They've found Parkar's and his mother's bodies buried at a construction site on the old Mumbai–Pune highway.'

Mirza sighed.

'Just as we'd feared,' he said.

'Yes, sir. Both of them shot in the heart. We believe one of them was shot inside Parkar's house and the other at the site. Possibly they shot his mother first. She must have been dead when she was seen being put inside the ambulance. They needed to keep him alive just in case some neighbour was awake. He needed to be seen while getting into the ambulance.'

'Probably shot him in the ambulance itself,' Mirza said.

'Yes. No one heard any gunshots, so it's safe to assume they used a silenced pistol. The shell casing in Parkar's house came from a .45 pistol.'

Mirza shook his head.

'Any other developments?'

'Yes, sir. The fellow we picked up? Wasim?'

'The auto driver who picked up the Kadir brothers' mother.'

'Right, sir. Wasim was recruited by a voice on the phone with a shitload of cash and never saw this man's face. I'm fairly sure he's telling the truth. But the house in Goregaon, where he was staying, it's in the name of one Abdul Jabbar Hakimi.'

Mirza froze. 'Why is that name familiar?'

'He's one of the captives on that cruise liner, sir. And according to the updates of the released hostages that you sent me, he's still there with Vikrant and the others.'

'Okay…' a puzzled Mirza said. 'That's … that's clever. Hakimi was on the cruise liner and his house would be the perfect place for Wasim to lie low.'

Mirza could hear Mankame sigh on the other end.

'Well, sir. We went through the details of the guests on board the cruise liner. The guests had submitted photos of themselves along with identity-proof documents. We compared Hakimi's picture from the cruise liner's list with some photos of him we found in Hakimi's house.'

Mirza felt a sudden sense of impending doom.

'It's not the same man?'

'It gets worse, sir. On a hunch, I compared the photo in the cruise liner's list with the one of Rishabh Chawla that we got from the hotel in Bhopal…'

'God almighty…' was all Mirza could say.

'The beard is gone and the hair is different, but … I think he's the man who posed as Rishabh Chawla in Bhopal.'

Mirza gripped the phone tightly as his heart started racing.

'Munafiq,' he said.

Goyal and Jaiswal's heads shot up.

'I'm afraid so, sir,' Mankame said.

'You're sure?' he asked.

'Yes, sir.'

'Find the real Hakimi,' Mirza said, thinking fast. 'Find his family. Talk to his neighbours. Get everything you can and get it yesterday.'

He ended the call without waiting for a response and stormed out of the room, Goyal and Jaiswal on his heels.

Five minutes later, he was filling in everyone in the Officers' Room on the developments.

'But ... but then ... then that means...' Mishra sputtered.

A senior IB officer cut him short. 'That means that one of the most dangerous terrorists we know is on that cruise liner, among the captives, aware of whatever Vikrant is planning along with Fernando.'

'It means we're fucked,' Mirza said sourly. Akhilesh Mishra sank into a chair and reached for a bottle of water.

'What should we do?' Shaina asked.

'Inform the PMO. And start exploring options to storm the cruise liner,' Mirza said firmly.

Mishra opened his mouth to protest but at that instant, a naval officer came running into the room.

'We think we hear gunfire from the cruise liner, sir,' the officer said, and everyone went running to the deck.

'You see anything yet?' the naval commander puffed into his wireless. One of his officers, who was still viewing the live feed of the cruise liner in the Officers' Room, answered in the negative.

Up on the deck, they heard a series of muted booms, which sounded very much like shots fired from Uzis. A long silence followed.

'Call Marwan,' Mirza said to no one in particular. The naval commander dialled the number and handed the phone to him.

The phone kept ringing till it rang out but there was no answer. Mirza dialled again; it still kept ringing. He was about to give up when the call was answered.

'What's happening there?' Mirza demanded.

'Keep watching the top deck,' Marwan's deep voice said at the other end before he hung up.

Half of the people on the aircraft carrier's deck went back to the Officers' Room, including Goyal and Jaiswal. Mirza and Shaina stayed, each holding a pair of binoculars. Mirza glanced at Shaina and noticed that she was clutching the binoculars so tightly, her knuckles were white.

'I'm sure he's fine,' he told her softly.

They waited for more than half an hour before they saw movement on the cruise liner's deck. Vikrant and Daniel were dragged up into open view by two Somali mercenaries and thrown onto chairs. Their hands and legs were bound to the chairs and they were left alone while the henchmen went down again.

Mirza and Shaina zoomed in and saw that Vikrant and Daniel were bleeding from several cuts on their faces. An ugly bruise was forming under Daniel's left eye. Vikrant, from the way he was shifting around in his chair, looked like he had been punched in the gut and was still hurting.

'What the fuck did you boys do?' Mirza said under his breath. Shaina turned around and walked away.

The mercenaries returned with Captain Rajeshwar Sahani and another young girl who, according to the roster that Mirza had examined earlier, was a Mumbai resident named Vaishali Sharma. She, too, was pushed onto a chair and tied up.

Sahani, on the other hand, was kept standing. His uniform was soiled and he looked like he hadn't shaved for several days.

Next, Marco came up and joined his five henchmen, who were standing to one side after dragging Sahani and Vaishali up to the deck. He was followed by Marwan and the IM Five.

'You guys seeing this?' Mirza said into his wireless and the naval commander, who was in the Officers' Room, replied in the affirmative.

Marwan marched Sahani to the edge of the deck. Taking a step back, he pulled out a pistol from his hip holster, pointed it at the back of Sahani's head and pulled the trigger. Everyone on the aircraft carrier watched horrified as Sahani was thrown forward and he fell off, straight into the sea.

# 42

*Wednesday late morning, Lakshadweep.*

'It's Marwan,' the naval commander's voice crackled on Mirza's wireless. 'He's asking for you.'

Quickly, Mirza walked down to the Officers' Room, where the phone was set on speaker mode.

'I'm here. What happened?' he asked.

'Your protégé and Fernando, who we gather is an ex-soldier, tried to stage a hostile takeover. Lives were lost on both sides.'

'Where are the other captives?' Mirza demanded.

'All dead. A middle-aged man, a young girl and an old man. They're all dead.'

'No, they're not,' Mirza said.

There was a silence.

'The real Hakimi never made it to the cruise liner. I don't know what you call the man who has been posing as him. But I have a good idea who he is. So tell him that Shahwaz Ali Mirza wants to speak to him.'

Everyone in the room watched the screen intently as Marwan turned and said something to Marco. The mercenary went below deck and returned two minutes later with a silver-haired man dressed in a simple shirt and trousers. He took the phone from Marwan's hand and Mirza couldn't help but notice that the younger man's demeanour was very respectful.

'Mirza,' the man said, putting the phone to his ear.

'Munafiq,' Mirza responded, and Munafiq grinned.

'Yes, I know that's what you call me. Quite a nice name, in fact. You thought of it?'

'Yes.'

'Come up to the deck, will you? It would be nice to see you.'

Mirza picked up the phone and headed to the deck, followed by everyone else. He walked up to the edge of the deck and Munafiq followed suit on the liner.

'So, you finally caught on,' Munafiq said. 'Too bad your boy wasn't as bright. But then … I am good at this.'

'Need these?' Shaina asked Mirza, holding up a pair of binoculars. Mirza took them from her and raised them to his eyes. He stared intently at the man standing on the deck across the water. He was solidly built and despite the fact that he seemed to be over fifty, Mirza had no doubt that he would be able to hold his own in a fight.

He recalled the photograph of Rishabh Chawla that his team had got from the hotel in Bhopal. As Mankame said, the beard that 'Rishabh Chawla' had sported in Bhopal was now gone. The hair, which had been thick and salt-and-pepper then, was now sparse and silver. Chawla had also had a mole on the left side of his face which, although not too prominent, stayed in one's memory. It was one of the oldest tricks in the art of disguise.

'It was you, wasn't it? Rishabh Chawla?' Mirza said into the phone, lowering the binoculars.

'Yes,' Munafiq said. He was clearly savouring the moment. Mirza couldn't blame him. Munafiq had met his five soldiers right under the noses of the police, orchestrated a prison break and simultaneously planned a hijack and planted himself right in the middle of it.

'Where is the real Hakimi?' Mirza asked.

'Strange question,' Munafiq replied. 'There is so much else you could ask me. Why inquire about one old man?'

'Because if he's alive, I need to rescue him. And if he's dead, his family deserves to give him a proper burial. There is plenty of time for me to stoke your fucking ego,' Mirza snarled.

There was a moment's silence before Munafiq responded. 'You think you're better than me because you take such pains to be human. But you're not. We're all the same, Mirza. Soldiers for different masters, fighting for what we believe in. So go ahead and be a hero to Hakimi's family if that makes you feel good about yourself. It won't change the truth.'

'Don't you ever tire of that little speech?' Mirza asked. 'All the killing of innocents and brainwashing the gullible, and you think one little speech where you refer to yourself as a soldier justifies everything? What was the fault of the two hostages whom you people killed just now?'

Munafiq burst out laughing.

'You're not so different from that little adopted son of yours, are you? He punched a diplomat in the face because he let his heart rule instead of the mind. And here you are, raging at me in the middle of a hostage situation, for the same reason. It doesn't make you better, you know; it makes you worse.'

'I really couldn't care less what you think of me,' Mirza said furiously. 'Are you going to tell me where Hakimi is, or should I find him the way my men found Parkar's and his mother's bodies?'

'Yes, that was unfortunate,' Munafiq said after a long pause. 'And completely avoidable. But men like Parkar...'

'Are the real Musallam Imaan,' Mirza cut in. 'I don't know what carrot you dangled in front of him or what rhetoric about "Islam being in danger" you tried to feed him, but if you had to hold his mother captive to make him do your bidding, it means he wanted to kick you out on your butt. These are the men that Islam is proud of. And if that doesn't tell you what a son-of-a-bitch you are, nothing will.'

'If you're done teaching me what my religion stands for,' Munafiq said, 'let's get down to business. Vikrant and Daniel have tested my patience. But killing them is too small a punishment, so you will pay instead. We had earlier given you forty-eight hours to hand over Lakshadweep to us. Twenty-four have already passed. But instead of twenty-four more, you now only have twelve. And at the end of those twelve hours, I will start a fire in which the entire city of Mumbai will burn to the ground, and I'll also kill Vikrant, Daniel and Vaishali with my own hands. Then I'll be gone.'

'Not for long,' Mirza retorted.

'Excuse me?'

'I said, not for long. Because you've been a pain in the ass for far too long. And now I've seen your real face. And I'm going to fucking kill you if it's the last thing I do.'

'First, go find Abdul Jabbar Hakimi's body in the Kalwa creek,' Munafiq said and hung up.

# 43

*Wednesday late morning, cruise liner.*

'Try not to be too harsh on yourself, son,' Munafiq said to Daniel, who was staring at him with pure, unadulterated hatred. 'Better minds than yours have been taken in.'

'It was all planned, wasn't it?' Daniel asked through gritted teeth. 'The whole episode between Vaishali and the henchman?'

'Yes, my dear boy. Yes. I was supposed to assume charge of the hostages and keep them in line, to ensure no one did anything to throw a spanner in the works. But people prefer your type – you know, tall, dark and handsome with a brooding persona and a military background – as opposed to some boring old man. So I asked Marco to cause a little stir. The mercenary was acting on his instructions.'

'So he's not dead like we'd assumed?'

Munafiq shook his head.

'We sent him off the cruise liner in a dinghy the same night. Made some calls and arranged for him to be picked up at sea.'

'How were you passing orders to Marco after the hijack?' Vikrant asked, curious despite himself.

Munafiq pulled up one of the legs of his trousers to reveal a small basic-model cellphone taped to his calf using a Velcro strap.

'All I had to do was visit the loo and send out text messages.'

'All that…' Vaishali now managed to speak. 'All those things you said … about your childhood…'

'About losing my parents?' Munafiq said. 'Well, I did lose them. They were both tortured to death by RAW agents because they wouldn't give up information about the Pakistani ordnance factory where they worked.'

Vaishali looked from Daniel to Vikrant, shocked.

'He's lying,' she said.

Neither Daniel nor Vikrant responded. Daniel had spent half his career working on covert operations that the Indian government would never acknowledge. Vikrant had seen enough during his stint with the IB to know that espionage was a dirty game. He actually had an idea about the RAW operation that Munafiq mentioned, having heard about something similar from a RAW veteran he had briefly worked with.

'They won't deny it,' Munafiq said. 'They can't.'

'Where does this stop?' Vaishali said in a weak voice.

'It stops with the obliteration of every enemy of Islam,' Munafiq said, a glint of steel entering his eyes. 'It stops at a point where no one shall touch a Muslim again, because no one will dare to.'

Munafiq walked away, head held high, towards Marwan and Marco. Marco's men moved closer to the edge of the deck to keep an eye on Vikrant, Daniel and Vaishali. The IM Five stood in a corner, talking among themselves.

'I'm going to kill the old fuck if it's the last thing I do,' Daniel said venomously.

'Cool it, Dan,' Vikrant said. 'I need you to be calm. I can't do this alone.'

'Do what the fuck alone?' Daniel asked savagely.

'Dan...' Vaishali said, sounding scared. She had never seen him like this. 'Please.'

Daniel turned to her and his gaze softened. Vaishali calmed him down and soon, Vikrant could see him looking at her tenderly. He deliberately cleared his throat.

'What?' both Daniel and Vaishali asked self-consciously.

'End of the world as we know it and you two still get to have a moment.'

They both looked away, Vaishali blushing.

'You got someone?' Daniel asked. 'You know, waiting for you?'

Vikrant sighed.

'I don't know,' he said, thinking of the way Shaina had looked at him when he'd left the aircraft carrier. She hadn't said anything, but Vikrant had a feeling that she had wanted to. He knew what it probably was. The problem was that he had no idea what his response would have been.

'It's complicated, huh?' Vaishali asked with a slight smile.

'That's putting it mildly,' Vikrant replied.

'Can you swim, Toothpick?' Daniel asked, glancing at Marco's men to make sure they were out of earshot.

'What're you thinking?' Vikrant asked.

'If we can get free of these ropes,' Daniel said, 'all we have to do is jump overboard. We're the last hostages left and with us gone, they lose leverage.'

Vikrant sighed again.

'Not exactly,' he said.

'What do you mean?' Vaishali asked.

'There's this little problem called the '93 Cache…'

Half an hour later, Daniel and Vaishali were looking at him with a mixture of shock and terror.

'Is that what Hakimi … is that what he meant when he said he would start a fire that would burn down all of Mumbai?'

Vikrant nodded morosely. 'And his name is Munafiq. I mean, that's what we call him.'

'Munafiq?' Vaishali asked.

'The Urdu word for two-faced.'

'Apt,' Daniel said. 'Why didn't you tell us about this cache earlier?'

Vikrant shrugged. 'There were too many scared people around us when I came aboard. I didn't want to add to the panic. Plus, I didn't know whom I could trust. I mean, I've worked with you before, Dan, but I didn't know anyone else.'

'And now?' Vaishali asked.

'Now,' Vikrant said looking first at her and then at Daniel, 'I guess it's the three of us for each other.'

'Damn right,' Daniel said. 'And this changes the stakes. We can't do anything without ensuring that they won't trigger an attack in Mumbai. Fuck knows what they've planned.'

The sudden noise of a jet engine distracted them, and they looked up to see a fighter jet descending onto the aircraft carrier.

On the other side of the deck, Munafiq heard the noise too. He quickly raised his satellite phone and had a brief conversation. Daniel assumed that he was speaking to someone on the aircraft carrier to ask what was going on. The response seemed to satisfy him, as he smiled a little before hanging up.

Vikrant, on the other hand, had been squinting intently at the aircraft carrier. As Daniel turned towards him, he saw Vikrant sporting a faint smile of his own.

'What?' Daniel asked.

'I think I saw Mirza getting on that jet,' Vikrant said.

'And that makes you happy because?'

'Mirza would never leave in the middle of a situation like this unless he had a really good reason.'

# 44

Prime Minister Parmeshwar Naidu stepped into the private bathroom in his office and went to the washbasin. He splashed cold water on his face again and again. Then he left the tap running while he stood, his hands clutching the sides of the basin, head bowed, water dripping from his face.

For a wonderful minute, his mind went blank. Then the chaos of multiple thoughts started again. The hijack, the demand, the update that he had just received from Lakshadweep.

The news media had hired private boats and were camping on the water as close to the cruise liner as the navy would allow. One boat had broken through the navy cordon and tried to get closer. It was immediately surrounded by naval boats, after which the journalists on board as well as the marine pilot were taken into custody.

Still, the media boats had been close enough to capture Captain Sahani being shot in the head and plummeting into

207

the water. At least two news channels were playing the scene on loop, and others were sure to follow.

The law-and-order situation in Mumbai was getting worse, Maharashtra Chief Minister Yashwant Pradhan had informed him, with people now abandoning their vehicles on the roads so that they could leave the city on foot. The highways were lined with abandoned cars, which the police were struggling to move.

The fanatics were having a field day, holding religious meetings and assuring anyone who would listen that their God would protect all those who embraced their faith immediately. Some of these fanatics were even on television news debates.

The situation was getting worse in Lakshadweep as well. The administrator, Danish Khan, had called Naidu half an hour ago to tell him that his office was flooded with calls from people asking what the government intended to do about the hijackers' demands. There was also talk of a massive protest being organized outside Khan's office.

'With all due respect, sir, if the government does decide to give in to the terrorists, I'd rather get shot on live television,' Khan had said before hanging up.

Naidu shook his head, turned off the tap and straightened up. Carefully, he dried his face and hands, discarded the towel carelessly on the floor and walked out to his office.

He made it halfway to his desk before stopping in his tracks. It took a good two minutes of staring at the man leaning against his desk before Naidu could believe that he was not hallucinating.

'What on earth, Mirza?' Naidu asked.

Mirza came forward.

'I was kind of going to ask you the same thing, sir,' he said grimly.

'How did you even get in here?'

'Does it really matter, sir?'

Naidu was silent for a minute.

'What do you want?' he asked, looking away from Mirza.

'The real question,' Mirza replied, 'is what do they want?'

He saw Naidu hang his head, and his heart sank. He was right.

It was during a brainstorming session with the others on board the aircraft carrier, in which he'd found himself wishing that Vikrant were with him, that a thought had stuck Mirza. It was something that a naval officer had said.

'How are they even going to keep the islands under their control?' the officer had asked. 'There are, what, ten of them now? Fifteen? We don't know how many of their men were killed by Vikrant and Fernando. They must have some kind of plan.'

'What about through INS *Dweeprakshak*?' Akhilesh Mishra asked, but the naval commander immediately shook his head.

'They can't control it without access codes. Any attempt at hacking and the base will shut down.'

'Still,' Mishra said. 'Let's keep that option open. Maybe that is the next thing they'll ask for after we surrender Lakshadweep to them.'

'*If* we surrender it to them,' Mirza snapped and Mishra's face flushed. Mirza would have said more, but then the idea had struck him out of nowhere. He took the naval commander aside for a brief conversation, after which he went to the room that he, Goyal and Jaiswal were using. Going through the heap of documents on the desk, he quickly pulled out what he needed. Then he called his friends in the IB.

Half an hour later, Mirza boarded the jet while the naval commander told Munafiq on the phone that the PM had called an emergency meeting, and Mirza, as the one who had been negotiating all along, had been ordered to attend it.

'How did you know?' Naidu asked Mirza, still looking away.

'The naval commander told me that you're one of the few people who has access codes to the naval mainframe. A mainframe that can be accessed from naval bases, like the INS *Dweeprakshak*. And I had to wonder why, when Daniel Fernando tried to include Vaishali Sharma among the hostages to be released, Marco himself intervened and insisted that she would stay. The other hostages I spoke to found it strange.'

Naidu said nothing.

'She hates you, doesn't she? Even uses her mother's maiden name.'

Naidu turned around. His eyes were glistening with tears.

'She's the only family I have left, Mirza,' he said, his voice breaking. 'I can't let her die. Not after what I did to her mother.'

Mirza took a deep breath.

'Sir,' he said fervently. 'Please tell me you haven't already given them the access codes.'

# 45

As Mirza ran to the fighter jet at the Palam Air Force base, which was already waiting, he felt as if his mind was in a whirl.

*Naidu isn't a bad person*, he thought, recalling the story the PM had narrated, as he jumped aboard and buckled in.

Thirty years ago, Naidu was a newly appointed regional party president from Bangalore. In the eyes of everyone around him, he was a young man with a spotless reputation and a bright future ahead of him. What no one knew at the time was that he was also father to a six-month-old girl, thanks a night of indiscretion.

Vaishali's mother Divya was a dedicated party worker. During an election rally which Naidu was leading, they had got closer than they intended to. When she became pregnant, she could not bring herself to kill her unborn child. Naidu had made it clear that he had national ambitions and was not going to let marriage slow him down, and Divya would have to live with that. He made her relocate to Mumbai and set her up in a flat, while she told her neighbours that she was a widow.

Every month, Naidu would send as much money as he could so that Divya and Vaishali's needs were taken care of. He would even visit Divya discreetly when he was in Mumbai. Vaishali met him several times and grew up looking forward to his visits, as he always brought a lot of gifts and goodies, but she did not know who he really was.

When Vaishali was twenty, Divya told her the truth about her father. She reacted by telling her mother to stop taking his money from that day onwards. The next time Naidu came visiting, Vaishali told him to go away and never return.

'You made your choice twenty years ago, Mr Naidu,' she said before shutting the door in his face. 'Nothing you do can change it now.'

Over the next seven years, till he was elected PM, Naidu made several attempts to contact Divya and Vaishali, but in vain. After his election three years earlier, he asked an IB officer, who was part of an elite cell reporting directly to him, to keep checking on them. The officer would give him periodic updates, including when Divya started suffering from heart problems and ultimately died of cardiac arrest.

'And then there is that cache from 1993,' Naidu had finished his story, wiping his tears. 'They're offering to give me back my daughter and leave Mumbai unharmed. How do I not obey them?'

Mirza thought hard and fast.

'They'll still need to get into *Dweeprakshak* before they can use the codes,' he said.

Naidu nodded.

'They will call off the attack on Mumbai the minute they have control of Lakshadweep. I have been told to clear every police and naval officer from Kavaratti so that they can take control unhindered. Then they'll give me the locations of some places where they have planted bombs, while their men, who are prepared to attack key locations in the city with assault rifles and grenades, will simply disappear. The entire cache will be ours to seize,' he said.

'What happens next?'

'They enter *Dweeprakshak* and take Vaishali and the others to the edge of Kavaratti under armed escort. Once they have access, they will call off the escort and let them leave the island.'

'And you believe them?' Mirza asked.

'I don't have a choice, Mirza. I'm not the one holding all the cards.'

'You have a few aces up your sleeve, sir,' Mirza said. 'A whole pack of aces, led by me.'

'I can't risk it,' Naidu said. 'As much as it kills me, I have to comply with them.'

Mirza stood up.

'I'm not giving you a choice, sir,' he said. He pulled out his cellphone and put it to his ear.

'You got all that?' he asked.

'My God! I mean, yes, sir,' a shell-shocked Mankame said from Mumbai.

'Make multiple copies,' Mirza said before ending the call. He looked up at Naidu, who was staring at him, terrified.

'What the hell have you done, Mirza?' he asked, trembling.

Mirza looked at Naidu silently as the old man walked shakily to his chair and sat down.

'How much do you trust me, sir?' he asked the PM.

Naidu just shook his head bitterly.

'I'm serious. You've seen my work. You know me. If I told you I had a way to get Vaishali and everyone else back safely, would you trust me?'

'You have a way of doing that?' the PM asked hopefully.

'I have one chance,' Mirza said, looking at his watch. 'We are seven hours away from the deadline they've given us. Give me six.'

Naidu stared at Mirza for a long time before looking away.

'Like you said,' he replied. 'You're not giving me a choice.'

Half an hour later, Mirza walked out of Naidu's office and called Shaina on the aircraft carrier and had a brief conversation, after which he asked her to put Goyal on the line.

'I don't care if you don't understand, lad,' he told a flummoxed Goyal after relaying his instructions. 'Just get it done.'

Then he ran to the helipad in the PMO compound, where a chopper was waiting to take him to the air-force base.

*You better know what you're doing, boy,* he thought, recalling the conversation he had had with Vikrant in private before turning him over to the hijackers.

# 46

*Wednesday evening, Lakshadweep.*

One of the basic lessons that Vikrant had been taught about crime and investigation was the value of foresight. Everyone that Vikrant had learned under, from his instructors at the IPS training academy in Hyderabad to the many officers that he worked with, including Mirza, had drilled into him how important it was to always think ahead.

'Not one, not two, as many steps as you can. You register a case, you think of the arrest. You make an arrest, you think of the investigation. You start drafting a charge sheet, you think about the conviction. Everything is always about the future,' one of his instructors had told him.

After being posted to the Maharashtra Anti-Terrorism Squad as a DCP, years before 26/11, Vikrant had attended a training session where Mirza was one of the speakers. That was when the future mentor and protégé had first met.

'Where there is terrorism, there is espionage,' Mirza had said in his talk as a roomful of young officers from anti-terrorism agencies from across the country listened intently. 'No one you arrest will simply be a foot soldier of a terror module. He will be a rung, a doorway for you into the module. Play your cards right and at least one of them will lead you across the border, where our friendly neighbourhood nemesis, the ISI, pulls the strings. That is a fight you win not with your fists, but with your brains. And that is where patience comes in. Because if you play your cards right, success will surely come, even if it's at the eleventh hour.'

The IM Five bust hadn't been Vikrant's work alone, although very few knew that. The IB had picked up some intelligence which they had passed on to the Maharashtra ATS, and the ATS chief had put Vikrant on the job. Vikrant had spent three months patiently watching the module and gathering every piece of information about them before he made his move. The result was a perfectly handled arrest operation and a water-tight chargesheet.

The same IM module now walked up to the deck as dusk started to break over the horizon. Vikrant watched as Qureshi, Mazhar Khan, Shaukat Asad, and Mustafa and Ibrahim Kadri assembled on the top deck, frequently turning his eyes to glance at the aircraft carrier.

The IM Five stood with their backs straight and their chests puffed with pride as Marwan handed out M16 assault rifles, Glock pistols, stiletto daggers and ammunition clips to each of them from a crate that Marco was holding.

Munafiq looked at them with the pride of a father as they loaded up.

'You have come a long way, my sons,' he said, his silver hair flying in the wind. 'From the time that I laid my eyes on you, I knew I had found the right people for the cause. You will spearhead our takeover of these islands, which will mark the beginning of a new chapter in our jihaad.'

Vikrant, who had at the time been staring intently at the aircraft carrier across the water, burst out laughing. Everyone turned to look at him.

'What the hell are you doing, Toothpick?' Daniel breathed.

'Just play along,' Vikrant whispered.

'You have something to say, you kafir?' Munafiq asked.

'I would…' Vikrant chortled. 'I would … if I could … stop laughing…'

'Share the joke, will you?' Daniel said loud enough for everyone else to hear.

Munafiq and Marwan made a movement towards them but Mazhar Khan, the burliest of the IM Five, beat them to it.

'Shut up,' he snarled, planting his huge frame in front of Vikrant.

Vikrant stopped laughing to stare insolently at the hulking terrorist. Taking a deep breath, he started talking. 'Your godfather met you at the Bhopal court posing as advocate Rishabh Chawla. He told you to break out of prison within a certain deadline and made getaway vehicles and weapons available. The vehicle you were in, when we had that encounter in Palghar, was parked somewhere in the vicinity of the jail itself. Am I right so far?'

Khan said nothing. Munafiq and Marwan, with the rest of the IM Five, stood in the middle of the deck, listening, while Marco and his five mercenaries stood near the railing, guns ready.

'You made a key using a toothbrush and you,' he said to Mazhar directly, 'opened your cell door and broke the guard's neck. It was you, wasn't it?'

Khan's snarl deepened but he still said nothing.

'What's your point?' Marwan asked.

'That I'm not stupid. And because I'm not stupid, I know exactly what's going on.'

'Which is?' Marco asked with amused curiosity.

'You,' Vikrant said to Khan, 'and your four brothers are being played. Don't you see? They're walking away from here, leaving you feeling like you are being given the greatest gift in the world, while they are actually leaving you to die.'

'Ah…' Daniel said with a smile.

'Yeah. Do you really think the government is going to hand over Lakshadweep to you guys? And do you think the five of you are going to rule over the islands like some kings? You'll be snuffed out in a minute, while your masters here get to safety.'

Daniel started sniggering.

'You're not the chosen ones, motherfuckers,' Vikrant said, laughing again, with Daniel joining in. 'You're the fall guys.'

Mazhar slid his stiletto dagger from its scabbard and went behind Vikrant. Clutching his hair, he brought the dagger to Vikrant's throat.

'If you don't stop laughing right now,' he said savagely, 'I'm going to slit your throat.'

Vikrant looked up, straight into Khan's snarling face. Then he winked.

In one quick movement, Khan moved the dagger across Vikrant's throat and brought it to rest by his side.

# 47

*Wednesday evening, Lakshadweep.*

Mirza's jet was about to begin its descent onto the aircraft carrier when the pilot jolted him out of his thoughts.

'Sir, I think you should see this,' he said.

Mirza leaned forward and peered through the windscreen. The jet was still high up, but there was apparent commotion on the top deck of the cruise liner and an unmistakable muzzle flash from at least two guns.

'Get me there,' he told the pilot. 'Get me on the bloody cruise liner right now!'

Goyal was waiting anxiously on the aircraft carrier. After getting off the phone with Mirza, he had spoken briefly to Jaiswal and then gone onto the deck, binoculars in hand. He'd watched intently as Marco's men milled about keeping an eye on Daniel, Vaishali and Vikrant and also looking at the aircraft carrier in

220

turns. At all times, someone or the other among the hostiles had an eye on the aircraft carrier.

'All you need is one moment,' Mirza had told him. Goyal watched without blinking, praying hard, till the moment came. The IM Five marched up to the deck and Munafiq went to address them as Marwan handed out weapons from a crate that Marco was carrying. Marco's men turned to watch, half-turning their backs to the aircraft carrier.

Goyal zoomed the binoculars onto Vikrant's face, who was staring directly at him unblinkingly from across the water. Quickly, Goyal pulled out a flashlight from his pocket, flicked it on, let it remain for three to four seconds and then switched it off. Vikrant smiled and winked, and Goyal heaved a sigh of relief.

He ran down to the Officers' Room, where the naval commander and several other officers were watching the confrontation between Vikrant and Mazhar Khan. He looked around to see Shaina peep into the room. She winked at him and slipped out again.

'Is that ... wait ... what the hell is happening?' the naval commander asked, staring at the screen, his eyes wide.

Only Daniel noticed that Khan's blade had never touched Vikrant's skin, passing barely an inch away. For two seconds everyone, from Vaishali to Marco and his men to Munafiq, Marwan and their four soldiers, were focused on Vikrant's throat, expecting to see blood spurt out.

In the same crucial two seconds, Khan slipped his dagger between the rope binding Vikrant's hands and slit it.

Everyone else was just starting to realize that something was wrong when Khan shoved his Glock into Vikrant's hands. Turning towards the IM terrorists, Khan then let loose a spray of automatic fire, catching Mustafa and Ibrahim Kadir square in their chests, while Vikrant opened fire at Marco and his men. Marco leaped out of Vikrant's line of fire, falling onto Munafiq, who, in turn, fell on Marwan.

Marco's men were not so lucky. Three of the five took pistol rounds from Vikrant in the chest and toppled over the railing. The other two raised their guns but their heads exploded in a mass of blood and brain before they could even aim.

Everyone on board looked around, confused, and Daniel was the first to notice Shaina standing on the deck of the aircraft carrier, a Dragunov sniper rifle in her hands.

'Hell, yeah!' Daniel said happily as Khan, taking advantage of the moment, quickly cut the ropes binding him and Vaishali. 'Stay down!' he whispered in Vaishali's ear.

Munafiq threw Marco off, grabbed Marwan and made a run for the other end of the deck.

'Cover us!' he yelled at Qureshi and Shaukat Asad, who reflexively fell into step, guns raised. They backed away, firing a couple of bursts, and found cover behind a row of deck chairs.

Marco came up cursing, his gun raised, but Daniel, snatching Khan's dagger, leaped at him and they both went down again.

Vikrant, meanwhile, untied the rope binding his feet and together, Vikrant, Vaishali and Khan crawled deeper into the cafeteria, taking cover behind a decorative fountain in the middle.

'You know where the cache is?' Vikrant yelled into Khan's ear as Khan fired bursts at Munafiq, Marwan, Qureshi and Asad.

'What cache?' Khan yelled back.

'The fucking weapons and bombs from '93!'

Khan looked at Vikrant.

'Don't worry about that.'

'What?' Vikrant asked.

'Trust me,' Khan said. 'Just put an end to this bloody thing.'

Vikrant nodded.

'Get her out of here,' he ordered. 'Go to the aircraft carrier. They'll be expecting you.'

Khan handed his weapon to Vikrant and dumped all his ammunition on the deck before wrapping a huge arm around Vaishali and dragging her to the far corner, away from the gunfire. Vikrant reloaded both the assault rifle and the pistol just as a jet came roaring close to the deck. He took one last look to check on Khan and Vaishali, and saw them go for the lifeboats.

Munafiq leaned forward and whispered to Marwan, who, in turn, said something to Qureshi and Asad. Marwan let loose a volley of rounds at the jet, which swerved away, while Asad and Qureshi opened fire at Vikrant, making him duck.

Then, almost together, all four ran to the railing and jumped over it. Munafiq and Marwan made it over the short distance and landed on the freighter that Marwan had come in on, which was anchored metres away from the cruise liner. Qureshi fell short but managed to grab the railing. Asad, however, was barely at the cruise liner's railing before Shaina cut him down with a well-aimed shot from her sniper rifle.

At the other end, Daniel and Marco were locked in deadly combat. Daniel, with one swipe of Khan's dagger, slit the strap of Marco's Uzi, which clattered to the ground. Marco tried to go for his Glock and Daniel kicked at his wrist, making it fall away as well. Daniel then charged ahead with his dagger raised, and Marco, in one easy movement, caught his wrist and twisted it.

Daniel held fast as Marco manoeuvred him to the railing, leaning hard. He kept pushing, making Daniel lean half over the railing, the dagger in his own hand inches away from the ex-soldier's face.

'Tough guy, eh?' Marco whispered in Daniel's face.

'Fuck you,' Daniel replied. In one quick jerk, he brought the dagger towards himself, letting it rip into his shoulder. The spray of blood in his eyes and the unexpected move threw Marco off balance, and Daniel fell backwards, toppling over the railing, taking Marco with him.

Across the water, Goyal, who was following the scuffle through his binoculars, followed the two men as they fell into the water. He would spend the next three months telling anyone who would listen that he had never seen anything like it.

'Fernando stabbed Marco in mid-air! He just pulled the dagger from his shoulder even as they were falling and rammed it up Marco's throat!' he would say.

On the freighter, Munafiq, Marwan and Qureshi were about to run into the lower levels. Qureshi placed himself in front of his two masters and let off a volley of shots to cover them. Vikrant ducked as the rounds chipped at the fountain, then sprang up and returned fire. Two of the rounds pierced Qureshi's chest, while the third blew part of his face away.

Munafiq pulled Marwan's pistol from its holster and they took positions back to back, guns raised, when three choppers from INS *Dweeprakshak* came roaring up into view, surrounding them from all sides. Mirza lowered himself from the jet onto the deck using a rope ladder, a pistol in hand. Vikrant sprang from his cover on the cruise liner and ran to the railing, coming to a stop parallel to the father and son.

For a moment, nobody moved. They all waited while the rotor blades of the choppers whirred. Vikrant glanced at Mirza, who was standing a few feet away from Munafiq, daring him to start something.

Then Munafiq stretched his hand sideways and let his gun fall to the floor. Marwan glanced behind him and, reluctantly, threw his M16 to the ground. They both stood, arms outstretched, as naval commandos lowered themselves on the deck. Vikrant clambered over the railing of the cruise liner and jumped aboard the freighter.

Mirza strode forward, gun by his side, till he was a foot away from Munafiq. Silently, Mirza stared at him, pure hatred blazing from his eyes.

Mirza was thinking about the day at the Ministry of External Affairs, which had started it all. He thought of Vikrant's conversation with Pakistan High Commissioner Zakir Abdul Khan before Vikrant had lost it and punched the diplomat in the face. He thought of the nine years of writing to the Pakistan government, the back and forth, all but begging for justice for the victims of 26/11. And he visualized a repeat of the entire process after Munafiq and Marwan's arrest.

Vikrant actually heard Mirza say, 'Fuck it' before his mentor raised his pistol and shot Munafiq in the face at point-blank range.

'NOOOOOO!' Marwan roared, diving for his gun. Vikrant stepped up, stood over Marwan and emptied the clip of his M16 into the son's body.

A group of impatient men waited as Khan and Vaishali were pulled up onto the deck of the aircraft carrier.

'Don't shoot,' Jaiswal yelled. 'Do not shoot the man!'

'Shut the fuck up already,' the naval commander barked at Jaiswal as Khan clambered aboard and was welcomed by several guns pointed at him.

'Where's the cache?' an IB officer snarled.

Khan sat down on the deck, feeling exhausted. Jaiswal pushed through the crowd.

'Where is the fucking cache?' he demanded.

'For God's sake!' a tired Khan said. 'There is no bloody cache.'

# 48

*Friday morning, New Delhi.*

Mazhar Khan stepped onto the balcony of the five-star hotel's suite and took a deep breath of the cool morning air.

'Mashallah,' he said to himself. 'It is good to be back.'

Khan's story wasn't a very unique one. It is similar to those of hundreds of young men growing up in the slums in Mumbai, drawn into the world of crime for one of the usual reasons. In Khan's case, it was rage.

Khan's mother, an attractive woman and the talk of many a boys-only party in the locality, had run away with a boy half her age when her son was fourteen years old. His father had coped by spending half the day smoking cannabis and the other half beating him and his ten-year-old brother Ayyub when they failed to earn enough money to fuel his addiction.

Khan had endured the abuse for three long years, channelling his rage by secretly working out at night at a local gym where he worked as a cleaner during the day, before he finally snapped.

One night, when his father came at Ayyub with a cricket bat, Khan, who had by then turned into a burly teenager, wrested the bat away and broke it into two with his bare hands.

'Next time you try to touch either of us,' he breathed in his stupefied father's face, 'I'll snap your spine like that.'

The threat, instead of putting some sense into his drug-addled brain, further enraged Khan's father. He sprang at his elder son and tried to strangle him and Khan, in one easy movement, caught hold of his father's forearm and fractured it in two pieces. He left the house with Ayyub, leaving the old man writhing on the ground.

As it was bound to, the law caught up with Khan, who was hiding at a relative's place, and he was taken to the local police station. His father had insisted on an FIR being filed and could not wait to see his son behind bars. The officer who had picked up Mazhar, however, took pity on him. He had seen too many products of broken homes and knew that putting them in juvenile homes was hardly the answer. And he had a feeling that the burly young man with the barely contained rage would end up taking a life in the juvenile home within his first month there.

The officer told his superiors that he could not find the boy and instead contacted Vikrant, whom he had worked with earlier. Vikrant, who was with the IB at the time, got one of his Mumbai-based informants to employ Khan in one of his godowns and would visit the boy from time to time, encouraging him to keep working out and making sure he wasn't straying, which was so easy to do at his age. Over the next four years, Vikrant and Khan became friends. Khan stayed at the same godown where he worked, while Ayyub stayed at a relative's place and attended a local municipal school. Khan made it a point to send money to the relative every month.

Then, without warning, Ayyub disappeared one day. Khan scoured the entire city for him but in vain. Two days later, however, Vikrant received a call from a cyber expert with the IB.

'Found a video of this kid saying he's denouncing the world for the higher purpose of jihad. He's from Mumbai, so take a look,' the cyber technician said. Vikrant watched the video and recognized Ayyub.

That was the last time anyone saw Ayyub. After a week, Mazhar Khan called up Vikrant and asked if they could meet. Vikrant agreed immediately.

'Ayyub was in touch with some fellows from the area who're involved with IM,' Mazhar told Vikrant.

'I'll get them picked up,' Vikrant assured him.

Khan shook his head. 'My fight is not with them. My fight is with the motherfuckers who mislead the Ayyubs of the world with their lies.'

Vikrant, for the first time, noticed that Khan was not the usual fireball of rage but deadly calm.

'What are you saying?'

'I want to go undercover. I want to infiltrate their module here and go as high as I can. I want to destroy the entire motherfucking chain.'

They had argued tooth and nail the entire night but at the end, Vikrant had had to give in. He had coached Khan on how to get noticed by the IM module, and ultimately, Mazhar was among the five young men who were handpicked and sent for training to Pakistan.

After the arrest of the IM Five, Vikrant, under the pretext of interrogation, spoke to Khan, and they decided that he would stay in jail till the case went to trial, just to pick up whatever else he could.

Then the jailbreak occurred and from that moment onwards, Mazhar and the others were constantly accompanied by someone or the other from the module, on orders from Munafiq. There was no way he could have contacted Vikrant, and Vikrant had guessed as much, which was why it was so important for him to get on the cruise liner himself.

Vikrant, on his part, had told no one about Mazhar, not wanting to risk the young man's life in any way. He had only told Mirza when they stepped out of the Officers' Room on the aircraft carrier, and Mirza looked ready to explode.

'Are you telling me that you've had a man among them all this bloody while?' Mirza said, struggling to keep his voice down.

Vikrant shrugged.

'Eleventh hour, remember?' he said.

'Boy...' Mirza began but Vikrant cut him short.

'Sir, please. There's no time. I need to get there and get in touch with him. Together, with him and Fernando, I can help put an end to this,' Vikrant told his mentor.

Mirza thought for a good two minutes before responding.

'I'm smelling something off here,' he finally said. 'Don't make a move till I signal you from here. We need to be sure we've got it under control from both sides.'

Now, as he stood on the balcony, Mazhar Khan smiled for the first time in years.

After the operation was officially declared under control, Vikrant, Daniel, Vaishali and Mazhar underwent a lengthy debriefing that went on all night. Vikrant was grilled for hours about Khan and Akhilesh Mishra even went as far as to state that Vikrant had made a mistake by not revealing earlier that he had a man on the inside. At which point Mirza had lost his patience.

'Exactly how many years of experience do you have in the field of espionage, Mister Whatever-the-fuck-your-name-is?' he asked bluntly, bringing his face inches away from the bureaucrat. Mishra realized that he was at a disadvantage, but everyone else in the room knew that his ego was going to get in the way of basic common sense. The naval commander was about to intervene when there was a knock on the door and Shaina poked her head in.

'We've finished searching the freighter,' she said.

'And?' the naval commander asked, welcoming the change of subject. Even Mirza moved away from Mishra and turned to listen to her.

'We found two DPVs and wetsuits to go with them in the hold,' Shaina said.

'Exit strategy,' Vikrant and Mirza said at the same time.

'Wait, what?' a confused Vaishali asked.

'Diver propulsion vehicles. Used for underwater navigation. They come equipped with breathing gas. Think scooter, but underwater,' Daniel explained to her as well as to an equally confused Mazhar.

'Wetsuits are suits worn underwater,' he added.

'Do we have DPVs?' the IB man asked.

'*We* don't,' the naval commander answered. 'The navy SEALs do, but several other countries manufacture them for recreational purposes. Quite easy to obtain.'

'That was their exit strategy,' Vikrant added. 'Munafiq and Marwan were going to slip away, leaving the others to die on Lakshadweep.'

'Motherfuckers,' Mazhar Khan said.

The rest of the debriefing went off relatively smoothly and soon, Mirza and his team, along with Vaishali, Daniel and Mazhar, were put on a plane and flown to Delhi, where they were all booked into massive suites at the government's expense.

'I'd suggest multiple suites,' Vikrant told Akhilesh Mishra. 'Some of us might want a little privacy.' He looked at Daniel and Vaishali. Daniel grinned and Vaishali blushed.

The PMO also booked the rooftop bar at the hotel, and Vikrant, Mirza, Daniel, Vaishali, Shaina, Goyal, Jaiswal and Mankame, who had flown down from Mumbai, got together that evening. The hotel manager was told to make sure they weren't lacking for anything.

For a short while, Mazhar found himself to be the centre of attention.

'Is there really no cache?' Jaiswal asked him, sounding disappointed.

'Well, if there is, I don't know where it is,' Mazhar said. 'But from what Marwan told us, it's all one big lie concocted by some bright motherfucker in the ISI way back in 1993, which was kept alive down the years.'

'That list?' Goyal asked.

'Marwan gave it to us. We were supposed to partly burn it and then plant it in that van.'

'What was the point?' Mankame wondered.

'Yeah,' Shaina chipped in. 'Why go through all this trouble?'

'Well,' Mirza said. 'Why not? It kept us chasing our own tails first, and then kept us scared enough. And the payoff? Access codes to the naval database through *Dweeprakshak*. They knew they were never going to be able to keep Lakshadweep. The plan was to leak all the navy's secrets to our friendly neighbour.'

'A plan that fell flat on its face, thanks in no small measure to Mazhar Khan,' Vikrant said from his end of the table. Daniel and Vaishali, who were sitting with him, raised their glasses enthusiastically and everyone else joined in, while Khan shifted in his seat and went red in the face.

The group partied till late in the night. Goyal and Jaiswal had to be escorted to their suite by Khan and Mirza, both teetotallers. Daniel, Vikrant and Mankame stumbled behind them, singing '*Ab tumhare hawale watan sathiyon*' together, completely out of tune. Vaishali and Shaina, reasonably in possession of their senses, followed them, shaking their heads at the 'boys'. Daniel and Vaishali retired to their suite, there was a separate one booked for Shaina and the rest of the 'boys' had a third suite for themselves.

And so it was that only Mazhar Khan and Mirza woke up early the next morning. Mirza joined Mazhar on the balcony and half an hour later, the two men offered namaaz together.

After that, they both sat down in the balcony with a pot of tea between them.

'What was the hardest part?' Mirza asked.

Khan looked away.

'Killing the guard,' he said. 'During the jailbreak. He was corrupt, abusive and communal to the core. But he didn't deserve to die.'

'You had to,' Mirza said softly.

'Yes,' Khan agreed. 'Qureshi told me that I had to kill him. Any reluctance on my part would have decreased their confidence in me. I did what I had to. It's not something I'm proud of.'

Mirza laid a hand on his shoulder.

'If it helps,' he said gently, 'some really evil men are dead because of you.'

The conversation continued till the others woke up and started filing into the balcony with hangovers of varying degrees.

'I'm giving you all two hours to make yourselves presentable,' Mirza told them. 'We've got one last thing to take care of.'

'Oh, yeah,' Vikrant said, rubbing his head. 'Let's finish this bloody thing already.'

# 49

*Friday afternoon, New Delhi.*

Mirza and his team, along with Daniel and Shaina, were felicitated at a special ceremony at the Prime Minister's Office premises, in the presence of the entire cabinet and senior officers from the armed forces as well as law enforcement and intelligence agencies. Also present were Maharashtra Chief Minister Yashwant Pradhan, State Home Minister Sudarshan Raskar, Maharashtra DGP Paramjeet Singh Kalra, Mumbai Police Commissioner Virendra Sinha and NIA chief T. Rangaswamy.

Prime Minister Parmeshwar Naidu shook Mirza's hands and held them for a long time before letting go.

'My pleasure, sir,' Mirza said. 'My pleasure.'

After practically blackmailing the prime minister of the country two days ago, Mirza had made him call Munafiq and tell him that he was ready to hand over Lakshadweep to him. This bit of deception was necessary to give Munafiq the illusion that he was in control so that when Mazhar finally revealed his identity, the surprise would have maximum impact.

'I'll be making a formal announcement in an hour,' Naidu had told Munafiq. 'I just wanted to let you know, as a show of good faith.'

Mirza had then sat with Naidu and made a list of false access codes to the naval database, which the latter could give Munafiq in case the need to stall for more time arose. Munafiq, in a rare display of overconfidence, had gathered the IM Five on the deck and started giving them a pep talk much earlier than anyone had imagined.

When Mirza called Shaina, he told her to be prepared to provide support to Vikrant and Daniel, and ordered Goyal to deliver the signal. He had also informed Goyal about Mazhar Khan, to make sure the double agent wasn't shot dead by some trigger-happy commando.

Naidu moved on to Vikrant, who was in uniform, and pinned a medal to his chest.

'Welcome back to the force, SP Vikrant Singh,' Naidu beamed, and Vikrant saluted him.

Next, Naidu walked up to Daniel, who had had his old army uniform flown up to Delhi on an SPG chopper for the occasion.

'Major Fernando,' he said. 'You have served the country even after discarding the uniform. There is no greater compliment I can offer a soldier.'

'I consider myself fortunate, sir,' Daniel said.

Naidu leaned closer.

'I am also happy that my daughter has found the right partner, and does not share my lousy judgement when it comes to making life choices,' he said softly.

'Thank you, sir,' Daniel said earnestly.

Naidu then presented medals to Goyal, Jaiswal, Mankame and Shaina.

'I'm told that the fine shooting out there is just one in the long list of your exploits, Major,' he said to Shaina, who beamed.

Everyone missed Mazhar and thought that he deserved a place of honour with them. However, they also realized that it was not possible.

Just before they'd left the hotel for the PMO, Mazhar had said his goodbyes. He was being spirited off to an undisclosed location, where he would begin life anew under a new identity.

Mazhar and Vikrant had hugged each other, and Vikrant thanked Mazhar for everything.

'You realize you'll always have a target painted on your back?' Vikrant asked.

'Frankly, sir, even if I'd died on that cruise liner, it would have still been worth it,' Mazhar said. The two men had parted ways with barely held back tears.

Now, everyone milled about, shaking hands and exchanging smiles. Naidu and Vaishali sat in a corner, talking earnestly. Mirza watched from a distance and nodded in satisfaction. They had a long way to go, but a beginning had been made.

Naidu stood up. 'Join us for tea, ladies and gentlemen,' he said to the guests of honour, taking Vaishali's hand.

Pradhan and Raskar went over to Naidu and had a short conversation, after which they left. Pradhan patted Vikrant's shoulder on his way out. Kalra and Sinha had already left. Rangaswamy went over to take his leave when Naidu said, 'Oh, Rangaswamy, join us for a second, won't you?'

The whole group trooped inside Naidu's office and made themselves comfortable around a large table on one side of the office. Mankame, who was the last one to enter, locked the door from inside and nodded to Mirza, who immediately went over to where Rangaswamy was sitting and pulled up a chair in front of him.

Rangaswamy looked at Mirza, then around him. Daniel and Vikrant were standing on either side of his chair, and Naidu was standing behind Mirza's chair, while the others were gathered around. Nobody looked happy.

Rangaswamy raised his eyebrows. Mirza sighed.

'The PM told me that after he got elected, he had asked an IB officer to check on Vaishali,' he said.

'And?' Rangaswamy asked.

'I didn't think of asking him who it was at the time. But later I got to thinking, how did Munafiq know something that even the PM's personal secretary didn't?'

Rangaswamy's face changed.

'You were in the IB back then...' Mirza said. 'I'm really praying to God that I've got this wrong, but you were the IB officer that the PM had asked...'

'Stop,' Rangaswamy said, looking at the floor.

Everyone waited as he struggled to find words.

'They ... they told me they were his political rivals... They said they... Some sort of political conspiracy...'

'So it was you,' Naidu said, looking furious. 'I mean, after all the trust...'

'How much did you get?' Mirza asked.

Rangaswamy winced.

'How much?' Mirza repeated.

'Fifty … fifty crore…'

'For fuck's sake, sir! After all those years working together?' Mirza was seething.

'It was … it set me up … my future… Being honest comes with a price, Mirza. And everyone around you pays that price,' Rangaswamy muttered.

Before anyone could see it coming, Mirza drew his fist back and punched Rangaswamy on the jaw.

# 50

*Friday evening, New Delhi.*

'So, RAW, huh?' Daniel asked as he blew smoke through his nostrils.

Vikrant puffed at his cigarette.

'Let's hope neither of us punches anyone,' he said, smirking.

Before they left his office, Naidu had told Mirza and Vikrant that he had recommended a posting in RAW for both of them. He also told Daniel that if he ever thought about rejoining the army, there would always be a place for him. Mirza, being Mirza, had drawn Daniel aside half an hour later and asked him to consider working as an asset for RAW.

'Yeah, well. At least your godfather didn't punch a diplomat from another country,' Daniel said, and both men laughed.

'Time to go, lads!' Mirza called out. The two men stubbed out their cigarettes and everyone walked into the Indira Gandhi International Airport in Delhi. The PM had made some calls and CRPF officers were waiting to usher them straight through.

They checked in their luggage and were led to the VIP lounge to wait till their flights were announced. They had all been booked into business class, courtesy of the Indian government.

Daniel and Vaishali had decided to travel together for a while to get to know each other 'under less stressful circumstances'.

'No cruises this time, please,' Daniel had told her.

Mirza, Vikrant and Mankame were going to Mumbai, where Mirza and Vikrant would wind up their pending work and move to RAW. Shaina, after seeing everyone off, would go to the NSG headquarters in Palam for a formal felicitation programme. Goyal and Jaiswal, meanwhile, were going back to the Bhopal office of the NIA.

Fifteen minutes later, the flight to Bhopal was announced. Goyal and Jaiswal shook hands with everyone and hugged Vikrant.

'Try not to fight, boys,' Mirza called out as they walked away.

Next, Daniel and Vaishali's flight to Coimbatore was announced. There was another round of handshakes and hugs that ended with Daniel and Vaishali both hugging Vikrant at the same time.

'You're a good person, Vikrant,' Vaishali said softly. 'Stay that way.'

Vikrant squeezed her shoulder.

'I'll see you around,' he told her, giving one of his rare smiles.

Turning to Daniel, he said, 'I'm really happy for the both of you. Something tells me you're making the right choice.'

'Speaking of choices...' Daniel said, gesturing with his eyes towards Shaina.

Vikrant merely nodded. Daniel stepped back.

'Look sharp, Toothpick.'

'Stay alive, Madman Dan.'

Daniel and Vaishali left hand in hand, waving goodbye.

Mankame spread himself out on a couch, replying to congratulatory messages from his peers back in Mumbai, while Mirza went back to exchanging gossip with spies across the world on his phone.

Vikrant headed over to Shaina.

'I never said thank you,' he said. 'You know, for that awesome sniper cover you provided.'

Shaina shrugged modestly.

'Just doing my part,' she said dismissively.

Vikrant took a deep breath but Shaina spoke before he could.

'Vikrant, I'm sorry,' she began. 'I'm really, really sorry. I led you on when I myself wasn't sure and then I just … I know it left you broken and I have spent so many days wishing I could take it all back…'

Vikrant let her finish.

'It's okay,' he said finally. 'Really, it is. You made the choice that made the most sense to you at the time. That's what we all do. That's what we all can do. So, yeah, it's okay.'

He patted her shoulder.

'Good luck,' he said. 'I hear you've got a great career ahead of you. I should know. I'm RAW.'

Both of them chuckled. Vikrant turned to walk back to his seat.

'Vikrant…' Shaina said hesitantly.

Vikrant turned again to face her.

'Can we … I mean … you want to catch up once I'm back in Mumbai?'

'Shaina,' Vikrant said after a pause, 'forgiving you is one thing. Trusting you or anyone again … that's not going to be so easy. I'm sorry, but there is no other way to say this.'

Shaina took it well.

'Fair enough,' she said.

At that moment, the flight to Mumbai was announced.

Shaina went over to shake hands with Mirza and Mankame, after which she came back to Vikrant.

'Stay out of trouble,' she told him.

'Nope. You stay safe.'

'Nope,' she said, returning his grin, and walked away.

Vikrant caught hold of Mankame's shoulder and led him towards the smoking zone.

'What the hell, boys?' Mirza grumbled.

'One last smoke,' Vikrant said, pulling out his pack.

'GODDAMMIT, lads!'

# Acknowledgements

*Eleventh Hour*, though fiction, is inspired by and derived from real-life events – a vast stash of RDX that has remained undiscovered since the serial blasts of 1993 and the Indian agencies totally clueless about it; the jailbreak in Bhopal of five men bound by a common mission; the hijacking of an Indian ship and a commercial vessel by Somali pirates and, of course, Pakistan's designs to spread terror in India and their intention to usurp Lakshadweep in 1947.

Since childhood, I was fascinated by men in uniform. At that time, I used to think that we could sleep peacefully because of all these heroes I would read about – men like Shahwaz Ali Mirza and Vikrant Singh.

This story had been in my mind for a long time. But I could not bounce it off my publishers or friends until it passed the first litmus test. My wife Velly and sons Ali Ammar and Ali Zain were surprised when, out of the blue, I took them out for a lavish dinner at my favourite joint in Andheri last year.

They not only approved the idea but also began discussing the twists and turns as they gorged on the food. Her Highness Velly Thevar, my strongest critic, put a seal of approval on the story, 'It will work.' In fact, she also started discussing the director and main characters for the movie adaptation!

Then I started the process of narrating it to my various friends from the police force and close associates in the intelligence community and adding more layers to the plot. The blueprint of the story was further strengthened with insights from my two young friends and pupils, Bilal Siddiqi and Gautam Mengle. Bilal, at the time, was too tied up with his own book *The Stardust Affair* and scripting the Netflix adaptation of his first book, *The Bard of Blood*. However, Gautam, a very fine journalist, became my sounding board and co-conspirator in the story. The book would not have been possible without his indefatigable contribution.

I am inclined towards non-fiction and consider it to be my core competence. So while writing fiction I am always plagued with massive self-doubts. When I hit a plateau, Ananth Padmanabhan gently nudged me to finish the book. I appreciate Diya Kar's work on the book as well. I would also like to thank my agent and friend, Kanishka Gupta, whose friendship I cherish.

However, my most special thanks in HarperCollins is reserved for Amrita Mukerji, my editor, for her calmness, patience and professionalism.